Clara's Courtship

J. Willis Sanders

BUGGS ISLAND BOOKS

Printed in the United States of America
Cover art by BookCoverZone.com

Reviews for *The Colors of Eliza Gray*
https://www.amazon.com/dp/B092RKPZBM

"Captivating! … J. Willis Sanders has captured love in this story. Love of a father to his daughter, love between brothers and sisters, and true love struggling to find a way to a future together. I look forward to Sanders' next book."

"I can honestly say that "The Colors of Eliza Gray" had me hooked from chapter one! It had me wishing for a "happily ever after" for Eliza from the beginning. Every emotion is found in this book and J. Willis Sanders definitely knows how to draw his readers in! I had read half of it before I realized it and finished it up the next morning!"

"Enjoyed this book so much! Stayed up way past my bedtime to finish it. Romantic and inspiring story. Great descriptions enabling the reader to visualize the scenes. Highly recommended."

"You won't be able to put this awesome book down! Love, love of a father and their love!!!! Please write another about how their lives are going!!!"

"The Colors of Eliza Gray is one of the most compelling books I've ever read. Beginning with a hearing-impaired abused Eliza. Taking you through her education and life altering experiences once she has her world opened to her. I truly hated it to end. Can't wait for the next book."

Reviews for *The Christmas Quilt: An Amish Christmas Carol*
https://www.amazon.com/gp/product/B0BNVQDKD1

"The Forgiveness Quilt is a wonderful book that can be read in one sitting or chapter by chapter. I took it with me on a long journey, and it made the trip so much more enjoyable. The book is well written and engaging throughout, with great descriptions of the setting as well as the characters. I highly recommend this as a pre-Christmas read!"

"This is the first book I have read by J. Willis Sanders but will not be the last. A very uplifting and inspiring book."

"In The Forgiveness Quilt, Sanders set a substantial challenge for himself: to recreate Charles Dickens' journey of writing A Christmas Carol in just six weeks. As a writer myself, I understand how challenging it can be to write just the first draft of story of this length in six weeks, let alone completing all the work necessary for refining the draft and preparing it for publication. With compelling characters, the sad journey of a heart hardening over time, immune to messages of love and joy, and its final, almost too late redemption, Sanders has succeeded in his challenge and created a moving holiday story of hope and redemption."

Reviews for The Outer Banks of North Carolina Series
https://www.amazon.com/gp/product/B098P67LJB

The Diary of Carlo Cipriani

"This is fascinating tale of survival, both of shipwrecked sailors and of how wild horses came to live on the Outer Banks. I enjoyed the characters and the character development, as well."

"The heartfelt descriptions of the characters brings them to life and bids you to follow their stories. There is life and love, despair and grief that eventually give way to hope for the future. A well written, intriguing story that bids me to learn more about the Outer Banks."

"Many twists and turns, lots of tragedy but always hope. At several points you are not sure what is real and what is the narrators madness due to his loneliness. A very satisfying resolution answers all our questions."

If the Sunrise Forgets Tomorrow

"What a captivating book. I read it in 2 sittings because we just couldn't put it down. Brought tears to my eyes!"

"This book was captivating and it was difficult for me to put it down. If you like a touch of history and have a love for Ocracoke, this is a great book to read. It was very descriptive and made me feel like I was there. Virginia and Ruby are typical sisters who are loving each other one minute and the next they are disagreeing. I enjoyed the strength they displayed as they overcame many obstacles. A Great Read!"

"To be honest, I wasn't certain I would enjoy this book. I've read other books at in the Outer Banks and a lot of them seem to be sloppily written and just capitalizing on the setting to prey on die-hard OBX readers. I was pleasantly surprised to find it very well written and descriptive. It was easy to visualize the island, the characters, and the story as it all unfolded. I would recommend checking it out!"

Reviews for *The Coincidence of Hope*
https://www.amazon.com/gp/product/B0B2KZ9KPM

"This is not war story, nor an action novel. It's not a love story. No, it's more than that, as it touches on many love stories, life stories, and stories of hope, as glimpsed through the thoughts of Joe's ghost. Excellent characterization, clever points of view. Revelations throughout the telling will surprise you. The story of hope that Sanders has created will grab you and keep you engrossed until the very end."

"Trust me when I saw you won't need a tissue but a whole box, this storyline really tugs at your heart and you won't be the same after reading it. I'm really looking forward to see where book 2 will take me. Give this book a change it's so very worth your time."

By J. Willis Sanders
Read more about his books at
https://jwillissanders.wixsite.com/writer

The Eliza Gray Series
The Colors of Eliza Gray
The Colors of Denver Andrews
The Colors of Tess Gray

The Forgiveness Quilt: An Amish Christmas Carol
The Easter Prayer: An Amish Easter Story

The Clara Engelman Series
Clara's Mourning
Clara's Courtship
Coming soon: *Clara's Choice*

The Essence of Emmaline Strong

The Outer Banks of North Carolina Series
The Diary of Carlo Cipriani
If the Sunrise Forgets Tomorrow
Love, Jake

The Hope Series
The Coincidence of Hope
The Yearning of Hope
The Gift of Hope

Writing as J. D. James
Reid Stone: Hard as Stone
Reid Stone: Red Rage

Readers: please enjoy the first chapter of *Clara's Choice* at the end of this book.

Dear readers,

The main character in this book is a young Beachy Amish Mennonite woman. There are many different Amish orders. One reason I chose this order is because they can use any technology except radios and television, which can lead to some interesting plot devices such as using cell phones and driving vehicles. A quick internet search of the Beachy Amish Mennonites shows why they don't use TV or radios, as well as the general rules they follow, also known as their Ordnung, which can vary greatly from community to community like with most Amish Ordnungs. Interestingly, according to research, they also don't speak Pennsylvania Dutch like most Amish do.

Although this book is fiction, I tried to write it accurately by researching it online and asking questions on online forums. Yes, all Amish value faith, family, and community, but I think we can be sure that life's challenges, just like anyone else's challenges, can cause turmoil in their lives.

The Amish and Mennonites are interesting people with admirable work ethics and dedication to God, and I enjoy writing about them in such a way as to make them have human frailties like the rest of us. After all, a good story includes conflicts like we all have. Since many of those conflicts happen when we search for someone to love, it's likely the Amish and Mennonites may experience the same thing depending on the individual and the circumstances, which is where the magic of fiction takes over. Yes, I'm smiling, because I dearly love the magic of fiction.

Also, if you've read my Eliza Gray series, you'll recognize some of the side characters in this book from that series. No doubt some readers of the series would like to get glimpses of their lives after the series ended, so this is why I chose to include them, as well as my hometown of Clarksville, Virginia, and the surrounding counties of Charlotte and Halifax and the town of South Boston.

If you'd like to visit a great website about the Beachy Amish Mennonites, here's the link: http://www.beachyam.org/

If you'd like to visit Clarksville online to learn about it and Kerr Lake, what us locals call Buggs Island Lake, visit https://clarksvilleva.com/#/

Thank you for reading,
J. Willis Sanders

Clara's Courtship

Chapter 1

Beside Clara in Abram's old pickup truck, Alison pointed at one of the pedals in the floor. "No, Clara. The one on the left is the clutch, not the brake. You let out on that one and push the accelerator at the same time."

Clara tried again, causing the truck to buck and bounce until it stalled. On the porch to her right, Edna and John cackled with laughter. Clara stuck her head out the truck window. "If I remember correctly, and I do, a certain young lady has her sixth birthday soon. If she wants pizza, she better stop cackling at her mama like a hen laying an egg."

"That's all right," Edna said, her cheeks red from laughing. "John's birthday is next month. We can have pizza then."

John smiled at Edna. "That's right, Edna. And Jonah can make strawberry ice cream."

Clara loved her children beyond measure. They were growing so fast. Not only would Edna be six soon, John would be five next month.

She pressed the clutch down and cranked the

truck. After a deep breath, she eased out on the clutch and pressed the accelerator at the same time. The truck moved forward as it should, unlike a bucking horse.

"Good job," Alison said. "You do fine on the road. If we can get you started without jarring my teeth out, you can get your license soon. Now try it in reverse."

Clara did so, glad she was improving. Edna would start school at Alison's home in three weeks, on the first of September, and Clara needed to drive her there by 8:30 every morning.

She stopped the truck and backed it past the porch, where Edna and John were clapping wildly. Clara took one hand off the steering wheel to wave, which made the truck swerve to the left. Alison grabbed the wheel. "Clara! Pay attention!"

Clara grabbed the wheel with both hands, happy she hadn't hit Alison's pickup parked to one side of the driveway. "I'm sorry. What do the English say about race car driving? I almost did that."

"'Swapping paint.' Don't you dare. Samuel just bought our truck. He wouldn't like a blue streak on the white paint."

Clara drove forward and backward a few more times. "I think I've got the hang of the clutch now."

She parked beside Alison's truck. As she started to get out, Alison grabbed her arm. "Whoa there.

Tell me when you plan to stop mourning and court Vernon. You've made him wait almost a year."

When Clara had called Alison to come for another driving lesson, she had expected this question to come up. Although her thoughts of Abram were more positive after more than a year without him, she sometimes broke down in tears late at night, when she woke from reaching for him in the bed and only found the empty place where he used to sleep.

Alison shoved her shoulder. "Stop ignoring me and answer my question. Oh, *I* know what it is," she said, waggling her finger at Clara. "You've got too many men to choose from—a handsome neighbor right next door and an old flame back in Pennsylvania, along with Vernon. How's Noah anyway? Has he called lately?"

"Yes, Miss Nosy," Clara said, uselessly trying to shame her best friend. "For an Amish woman, you like to ask personal questions."

"I ask because you won't tell me anything. Is Noah still thinking about buying some land around here? You know it's just to be near you. Maybe you could court Vernon a few months and court Noah a few months and decide who you want."

Ignoring Alison, Clara got out of the truck. Both Vernon and Noah were Beachy Amish Mennonite like her, but she didn't have the same feelings for them as she had for her neighbor, Jonah. Unfortunately, he wasn't any kind of Amish or Mennonite, so she had to constantly tell herself to stop thinking about him as a possible husband. Regardless, though, she *did* think about him as a possible husband. Not only did he understand her struggle with the decision to court Vernon when she didn't love him, he had been helping her with the farm ever since they met, more than a year ago. He had also saved Edna's life by taking her to the hospital in South Boston, when a Black Widow spider bit her. To Clara's astonishment, when a nurse had taken her to see Edna in intensive care for the first time, Jonah pretended to be her husband so he could go too, and he had cried when Edna, lying in the bed with a ventilator tube filling her small chest with air, woke up. Of the three men in her life, it was a shame how Clara couldn't court Jonah. They were as alike as her and Abram had been. She could count on him like she could count on God sending the rain in the spring to help the flowers bloom and her garden to grow.

On the way to the porch and the waiting children, Clara pulled Alison aside. "Stop your teasing about Jonah. I don't want John and Edna to get the wrong idea."

"Wrong idea?" Alison sputtered. "You're the

one with the wrong idea and you know it. Why don't you tell him how you feel? He might join our community so you two can be together."

"You have lost your mind," Clara said, leaving Alison.

On the porch, John and Edna clapped again. "When can we go to town?" Edna asked.

"Me too," John said. "I wanna pick my birthday present."

Clara climbed the steps and tousled his hair. "No, sir, it's a surprise. Besides, I explained how we give simple gifts instead of extravagant ones."

"What's 'stravagant?" John asked. "I just want a toy boat."

"Me too," Edna said. "We can play with them in the lake when Jonah takes us fishing again."

"My, my," Alison said from the bottom of the steps. "It must be nice to have someone like Jonah to take you fishing on the lake." She faced Clara. "Let me know when you want to take your driver test and I'll take you." She winked. "Unless Jonah can take you." She waved at John and Edna. "Make your mama behave, you two. See you later."

Edna tugged Clara's dress. "Why did she make that face at you, Mama? Did she have something in her eye?"

"That's called a wink," Clara said. "People do

that when they say silly things." She opened the door. "It's late and I need to cook supper. Both of you wash up so you can help."

"No, Mama," Edna said, pulling Clara's hand. "We haven't talked to Papa today."

Shame warmed Clara's cheeks. Without fail, unless weather intervened, she and the children had visited Abram's grave behind the house, beneath the huge limbs of an old oak tree. She apologized to Edna and told her and John to come along.

The sun shone brightly on them until they entered the shade. Edna went straight to the single white cross made of painted wood and touched it. "We're here, Papa." She looked up and waved. "I hope you're having a good day."

Having never seen Edna do this, John looked up too. "Is Papa in the tree? I thought he's in Heaven."

"He is," Clara said. "Edna's just waving to him through the tree."

John waved too. "Hi, Papa." He went to the cross and touched it, then faced Clara. "Will we ever have another papa? I want one to take us fishing like Jonah did that time."

"Me too," Edna said.

Clara said nothing. At least they hadn't mentioned having Jonah for a papa. As much as they enjoyed being with him, and he with them, it was a wonder.

Clara touched the cross and stepped back while the children told Abram about their day, plus their coming birthdays. They didn't say so, but she knew they wished he were here like she wished he were here.

It was hard to believe over a year had passed since his death. So much had happened since then too, including her miscarriage on the same day the spider had bitten Edna.

Although her family's community was over thirty minutes away by vehicle, they had taken up an offering to help her after Abram died. As grateful as Clara was for them, if the truth be told, she was more grateful for Jonah. Even with the puzzle of who Lydia was, the woman who lived with him, he and Clara had grown close over the past year. He had even driven her and the children to Pennsylvania last year around this time so they could visit Clara's and Abram's parents. During the visit, she had planned to ask her parent's permission to court Vernon when she felt like her mourning period was over. Then he had come there without telling her, right when she had come home from visiting Noah, who she had wanted to court when she was fifteen. That night, Jonah had called from his hotel room to see how she was. Knowing it was wrong, she had suggested they go for a drive. She had even left her hair down. They had parked near a creek, where she had broken down in tears. Typical for Jonah, with how he seemed to know her so well, he had told her she would have to make her own choices in life. Regardless, she had asked him to comfort her by holding her, but as best friends only. She had done so by crawling into his lap like a child, and he had held her like a child. Except for when Abram had held her, she had never felt so safe. What a blessing Jonah was. If he were part of their community like Alison had teased, Clara would court him in a heartbeat. Then again, the question of his and Lydia's true relationship stayed stuck in the back of Clara's mind as if it were a biscuit stuck in molasses.

The children's voices trailed off. They touched the cross and said goodbye to their papa. Yes, it was well over a year since he had died, but this scene still filled Clara's throat with emotion. After forcing it down with several hard swallows, she told the children to come along and wash up so they could cook supper.

As they walked through the grass that needed cutting one last time before frost, Clara prayed to God to help her through the next year like He had helped her through this one. He answered with His living presence, in the chickens scratching around the henhouse, in the milk cow grazing in the pasture, in the wilting garden that needed to be plowed under soon. He had met her needs and more since Abram had died. Now He would meet her needs with courting Vernon, so she could decide if he would be a suitable husband for her and a suitable father for Edna and John.

Unfortunately, no matter how hard Clara prayed for Vernon to be those things, whether during the day or at night, when she woke in tears because she missed Abram so much, she never felt the same calm assurance she felt when she prayed about other things.

Maybe this part of her life was a test of faith. She had surely failed her faith when she had crawled into Jonah's lap and allowed him to comfort her as if she were a child.

In the kitchen, she and the children washed their hands. While all three made a chicken casserole, rolls, green peas, and a blueberry cobbler with berries Vernon had bought from the grocery in South Boston, doubt crept into Clara's mind.

Where was her life taking her? She felt like a leaf in the wind: dried and brittle, about to be crushed under the weight of her coming choices, plus the desire to be a good mother to her children by finding them a father.

If only love could be found in that choice, but it wasn't meant to be.

Chapter 2

Excited about getting her driver's license, Clara returned Alison's wave as she backed her car out of the driveway. What a blessing her friend was for helping her. Now to drive to Jonah's house and surprise him.

In the pickup truck, Clara slammed the door harder than usual. She was driving to Jonah's to get the children, *not* to surprise *him*. She had planned to drive to Vernon's now and tell *him*. Shaking her head in frustration at her continued thoughts of her neighbor, she drove the short distance to his home, just beyond the hill between their houses.

To her right, in a pasture he had fenced last year, a herd of twenty-five Black Angus beef cattle grazed. Some switched their tails. The sun glistened on their black hides. The bull raised his head from the grass to appraise Clara's truck as she passed. She couldn't smell it with the window up, but when the wind blew toward her property, she and the children would catch the hint of manure.

She parked behind Jonah's huge, dual-wheeled

diesel pickup truck. Looking in the rear-view mirror, she tucked a few loose strands of hair, red and bright as a summer sunset, beneath her kapp.

Out of the truck, she pressed her hands along her sky-blue dress to remove the few wrinkles. The screen door beneath the porch of Jonah's house opened. Beaming a bright smile, he strode out to her, and Clara's couldn't help returning the smile. As attractive as Abram's smile had been, it still didn't compare to Jonah's smile. "Well, well," he said, stopping before her. "You drove here instead of walking. That must mean you passed your test."

Without thinking, Clara lightly slapped his arm. "Stop your teasing. I thought you had faith in me."

"I do. Vernon's the one who was worried."

Clara agreed but didn't say so. Vernon's ideas about the roles of Beachy Amish women were to let the men drive. Still, he understood how she needed to take Edna to school soon.

Behind Clara, the bull, evidenced by his deep voice, bellowed, and Jonah laughed. "I think someone's got love on his mind." He grabbed Clara's hand and rubbed her ring finger. "It's too bad the Amish don't give engagement rings. You could sell yours if Vernon gave you one and buy a pig for butchering next fall."

Clara snatched her hand away. "I think we already have a pig, and you know who I mean."

She squeezed Jonah's nose. "There's a hint if you need one. Oink."

He leaned against her truck. "It's good to see you smiling, Clara. You sure had a tough year. Do you think you and Vernon will court soon?"

Clara leaned against the truck too. "It sounds like you're in hurry to get rid of me."

"Not at all. He said he would move to your house if you got married." Jonah bumped her shoulder with his. "Besides, if you moved away, you'd miss me more than I would miss you."

With a half-smile, half-frown, Clara rolled her eyes at him. "I doubt that. You still have to wire my house for electricity and make all that money you'll charge me when you're done."

"Enough of our silliness," Jonah said, turning to face her. "We're good friends, so I don't think you mind me asking something personal. Have you decided how much longer you'll wait before you start courting Vernon?"

The memory of Jonah holding her that night in Pennsylvania tugged at Clara's heart. What a terrible thing, to know your choice and not be able to make it. *Dear Lord,* she prayed, *please help me stop thinking such things. I know I'm weak because I keep thinking about my feelings only. Help me concentrate on what John and Edna need instead of what I want.*

Jonah leaned over to look into her eyes. "Hey, Miss Green Eyes. That's a mighty serious look you have there."

"I … Well, I was going to drive to Vernon's and tell him about my license. What are John and Edna doing?"

"Lydia's making chocolate chip cookies." Through the screen door, a beeper sounded. "There's the first batch. Let's go have one with some milk."

Clara went with Jonah to the porch. The aroma of fresh-baked cookies drifted through the screen door. When Jonah opened it, John and Edna came running, their shoes pattering on the floor. "Mama, Mama! Did you pass the test?" they both yelled.

"I sure did," she said. "Do you want to go tell Vernon? I'd like to surprise him."

John took Clara's phone from her dress pocket and offered it to her. "Call him and tell him. I want my cookies warm."

"I'll wrap them for you," Lydia said.

"They're better from the oven," Edna said. She took the phone from John and offered it to Clara. "Here. You can call him later."

Drawn to the aroma of melted chocolate, Clara put the phone in her pocket. "Well, I still want to go after you eat your cookies. I thought you'd be excited to have me drive you somewhere."

Edna covered a giggle. "You might bounce us too much."

John nodded. "Like you did with Alison."

Clara sat at the kitchen table. Lydia brought a plate of cookies over. Jonah brought glasses of milk. "I saw your bouncing truck," he said, sitting beside Clara. "It's wonder you didn't get whiplash."

John and Edna asked what that was. Jonah explained it was when a person's neck got hurt from their head whipping back and forth. Satisfied with the explanation, they enjoyed cookies and milk, licking their lips and saying how good they were. Clara loved Jonah's patience with the children. Like Abram, he always took the time to explain things to them. Vernon, however, didn't, like the time they went fishing with Jonah and Lydia, had snapped at Edna when she threw a fish back that John had caught, saying he wanted to eat it. Still, he had apologized later, but it made Clara wonder what kind of father he would be. About to drink milk, she lowered the glass and took the vibrating phone from her pocket. Seeing it was Vernon, she told everyone she would outside to talk to him. Before she could tell him she had gotten her driver's license, he cleared his throat. "I'm sorry, but I won't be able to come to Edna's birthday party."

Clara waited for an explanation. Since he wanted to court her, plus be a father to the children, she deserved one for him missing such an important occasion. Instead, silence entered the conversation for several heartbeats. "Well," she finally said, adding a firm tone to her voice, "do I get to know why you're not coming to Edna's sixth birthday? It's important, not only to her but to me."

Vernon's breath sometimes whistled in his nose when something bothered him. It did so now. "I don't care to bother you with it."

"You already did. If you expect us to court and eventually marry, we should be honest with each other." Clara softened her voice. "Married couples share their burdens, Vernon. You should know that after being married yourself. If we're not honest with each other now, what does that say about our relationship?"

Vernon's nose whistled louder. "Oh, so I guess you believe the rumors about my wife divorcing me. I thought better of you than to believe gossip, Clara. Maybe we shouldn't court after all."

Clara had never known Vernon to be so defensive. Still, if he were going to act this way over a simple misunderstanding, maybe they shouldn't court at all. She started to tell him exactly that, but a choked sob came from the phone. "Vernon, what is it?" she asked, softening her voice even more.

Heavy breaths came from the phone, followed by the sound of him blowing his nose. "I'm … I didn't want to tell you this. Edna's birthday is the same date as when my wife died. I visit her grave then."

"You didn't mention it last year."

"We didn't get together for her birthday last year. We went out for pizza for John's birthday, remember?"

"Oh," Clara said, ashamed she had forgotten. "Will you be gone long?"

"I stayed a day last year. I'd like to stay two weeks and visit my friends in my old community. I also want to use the time to visit some other bishops to discuss changes to our Ordnung."

Vernon's reply puzzled Clara. No one in their community had mentioned changes to their Ordnung. Maybe the men kept it to themselves. It made sense. When was the last time the men asked the women their opinion on Beachy Amish doctrine? Of all their strict rules, leaving women out of such decisions troubled Clara the most. Such changes affected them, so they should be a part of the discussion. The next thing they knew, the men would have them doing nothing but staying home and cooking and cleaning and having children like farm animals. Her eyes widened. Wasn't that what they were doing now? *Dear Lord,* she prayed, *please forgive me for questioning our Ordnung. I know we follow our rules in order to be closer to you, and for the good of our families and our community, amen.*

Vernon cleared his throat. "I hope you understand, Clara."

"I do. Will I see you before you leave? We just had church yesterday, so we won't have it before Edna's birthday."

"No, I'm sorry, but I plan to pack and leave early. I might even stay three weeks. One of our men can hold church for one day."

Clara didn't know who that would be. The oldest man in their community had passed away three months ago. That left Samuel and a younger man. She decided not to worry about it. Let the men decide. That was their duty anyway. She told Vernon goodbye and to have a safe trip. As she spoke the words, relief washed over her like a cold rain. She would have three weeks to decide if she would court him or not.

Inside, she sat and took a cooling cookie from the plate. "Vernon's going away for three weeks, so he won't be here for your birthday, Edna."

About to drink milk, Jonah lowered the glass. "What do you think, Lydia? Should we invite a certain neighborhood family to join us?"

John and Edna whirled their faces toward Jonah.

"Where, fishing?" they both asked.

Jonah burst out laughing. "You two are a mess."

"I agree," Lydia said, "let's adopt them." She faced Clara. "You know I'm just teasing, but they're sweeter than my chocolate chip cookies."

"Not fishing," Jonah said, "but it's close, and we can go while we're there."

Edna screwed her face into a frown. "But where, Jonah?"

He faced Clara. "You mama has to agree before I tell you."

"I don't think I like the sound of this," Clara said. "For all I know, you'll take us camping and have a snake get us. I don't like snakes."

"We won't let a snake get you," Lydia said. "You're right, though, we're going camping, but in a cabin right on the lake in Occoneechee State Park."

In the middle of a bite of cookie, John swallowed. "Yay! It can by my birthday present."

"No, John," Edna said, pouting. "It's for *my* birthday."

The news pleased Clara. She could think of nothing better to do than watching the beautiful lake, especially as the sun set over the horizon beyond the picturesque town of Clarksville. She took a napkin from the holder and wiped chocolate from John's mouth, then faced Edna. "We'll share birthdays, sweetheart. That's okay, isn't it?"

Edna faced Jonah. "Can you make strawberry ice cream?"

"I sure can." Jonah faced Clara. "We've got plenty of food, so don't worry about—"

"No you don't, Lydia said, smiling at Clara. "I'd love to learn some authentic Amish recipes. I know a few, but not many."

Clara agreed to teach Lydia to cook whatever she'd like. Then they made more plans for the trip, like when they would leave and what they would do when they weren't fishing. Lydia said they could hike nature trails and visit Clarksville, but what she wanted most was to sit on the cabin's deck and relax by watching the lake.

Regardless of Clara's excitement, two things stuck in the back of her mind: would she and Jonah maintain their friendship instead of getting closer, and would she be able to discover if he and Lydia were brother and sister or if they were engaged? As soon as those thoughts popped into her mind, she chastised herself like she had earlier. She was about to commit to courting Vernon, so that had to be her focus, including the children, from now on.

Chapter 3

After unpacking the children's clothes, Clara told them to put them away in one of the dressers in the room they were using in the cabin. Beside one wall, two bunk beds waited for them later tonight; she would use a queen-size bed by the other wall. At the foot of her bed, as she put away the last of her clothes, a mirror over her dresser reflected tendrils of her red hair that had escaped the pins beneath her kapp. Despite the air conditioning, the hot August day caused sweat to darken the blue fabric of her dress beneath her underarms. In the adjoining bathroom, a large shower promised cool relief before bedtime.

John and Edna finished putting away their clothes. Clara followed them to the huge living room, the walls constructed of pine logs shining with dark varnish. At the other end of the room, two sliding glass doors with curtains tied back revealed a wooden deck. Beyond it, the shoreline of Kerr Lake, also known to locals as Buggs Island Lake according to Jonah, beckoned to vacationers.

About halfway across the huge expanse of water shimmering with sunlight, a pontoon boat motored by. Behind it, at the end of a length of rope, someone was being pulled on a round float.

John pointed. "What kind of fishing is that, Mama?"

Edna went to the sliding glass doors. "Are they chasing them?"

Putting away food in the adjoining kitchen, Lydia came over. "That person is riding that float for fun."

Edna raised a hand to shade her eyes. "It's a girl. Why's she only wearing underwear?"

"That's a bathing suit," Clara said. "We don't wear them."

"It looks cooler than our clothes," John said. He faced Clara. "What do we wear when we go swimming?"

Clara hadn't expected this question from her curious son. "We never went, so I never thought about it."

"They haven't vowed to be part of the church yet," Lydia said. "That means you can choose what they wear."

Regardless of this being true, Clara didn't want her children to swim half-naked. She told Lydia she had heard of Beachy Amish children wearing shorts and a T-shirt swimming, and she said they could shop in Clarksville for those items.

"Except," Jonah said, coming from his bedroom, the park doesn't have a swimming area. It does have a splash park, though."

"I wanna swim, not splash," John said. He poked his lips out. "I can splash in a puddle."

"There's a swimming area not far from here," Jonah said, patting John's shoulder. "We'll go."

"Can we go now?" Edna asked. "It's hot."

Lydia went to a thermostat and adjusted it. A vent in the floor at Clara's feet blew cold air up her dress, making her quickly step aside.

Jonah laughed. "Look at those wide eyes of yours. Someone likes air conditioning."

"And she'll love it even more whenever you install it and wire her house," Lydia said, affectionately rubbing his back.

Clara faced the lake again. For someone who claimed Jonah was her brother, Lydia often acted as if they weren't siblings. Although it wasn't any of Clara's business, she still wanted to know. If they were engaged, as one rumor by Alison had it, she could forget any possibility of marrying him, impossible as it was anyway since he wasn't Beachy Amish Mennonite.

* * *

Suppertime came and passed. Clara washed

dishes and thought of the day so far. Jonah and Lydia had cooked hot dogs and hamburgers on a small propane grill he had brought from home. Instead of french fries, Clara cooked fried potatoes and onions and bell peppers, one of the children's favorite dishes, in a pan on the electric stove inside. Jonah and Lydia enjoyed them too. Butter pecan ice cream from the grocery in town followed, surprising Clara. Who would've thought to make ice cream with nuts?

As the evening progressed, she considered the differences between her life and an English person's life, such as swimsuits that revealed more skin than she was comfortable showing, plus foods like hamburgers and hot dogs. Although she made meatloaf, her family had never tried ground beef in a patty or meat shaped like skinny sausage, both placed on a bun. To her, fresh tomatoes from her garden made the hamburgers much better, including lettuce and a slice of onion. Lydia didn't like onion, saying she didn't like how they made her breath smell. At her remark, Jonah, sitting beside her on the picnic table by the deck, had kissed her cheek and said her breath didn't bother him. She had responded by shoving him away, yet more confusing actions that didn't clearly define their relationship.

John and Edna had smacked their lips over the

hot dogs. Both ignored the mustard, relish, slaw, and chopped onions, choosing to eat them with ketchup. They also had loved the butter pecan ice cream, asking Clara if they could make ice cream with the acorns that fell each fall from the oak tree behind the house. After laughing, Jonah said that would be some bitter ice cream.

Clara finished the dishes. Lydia dried the last one and put it away. At the coffee table in the living room, Jonah was showing John and Edna a puzzle, found on a shelf for rainy days, Clara supposed.

She went to the sliding glass doors. The sun was on its downward slide toward the horizon. No boats motored by. Across the lake, lights were winking on in the distant shapes of houses tucked into the woods. Clara faced the sofa, where Lydia had joined in with the puzzle. They were so consumed with it, Clara left for the deck to sit in one of four chairs of what Jonah had called a patio set, complete with a huge umbrella and a table.

Other than the children and Abram when he was alive, Clara's one passion, other than her faith, of course, was the outdoors. Like a liquid magnet, the lake drew Clara as if she were liquid steel. The waves lapping on the shore, the silvery sheen of its surface, the breeze upon her cheeks with its watery aroma similar to a summer rain—each of those things calmed her to the point of making her drowsy.

"Clara?"

She knew that voice; Abram had come to her in a dream. His hand softly rested on her shoulder. Pressing her hand to his, she tearfully told him how much she missed him and how much she loved him. He said he understood. She said the children missed him too. He said they were growing up too fast, but he had been watching her, and he was proud of her for raising them so well.

A hand shook her shoulder. "Clara, everyone's gone to bed. Lydia helped the children get ready while you were sleeping. She was tired too, and we go to bed early at home."

Clara opened her eyes. Jonah was standing beside her, his hand on her shoulder. She wiped tears from her cheeks. "I'm sorry. I was dreaming about Abram."

When she stood, she saw it was almost dark. A single lamp burned inside the cabin, softly illuminating Jonah's face. He took her by the shoulders. "I'm not Abram, but I can hold you if you need to cry." His brown eyes shined like golden embers in the night. His concerned expression, no hint of a smile, caressed her heart as if it were one of Abram's gentle fingertips caressing her lips. Sobbing, she fell into his arms with shame—shame because her tears were more for knowing she cared for Jonah than for her fading memory of Abram.

He rubbed a circle between her shoulder blades, stopping now and then to press her into his chest. He smelled of smoke from the grill with a hint of fresh air. As her sobs ended, he pulled away to cup her cheeks in his palms and tilt her face toward his. "I wish I could bring Abram back for you and the children, but I can't. All I can do is hope you the best with Vernon."

When he had tilted her face toward his, Clara had hoped he would kiss her. Now his words were a hammer striking her heart.

She shoved him away and ran from the deck to stop at the shore of the lake. He followed her, evidenced by his shoes swishing in the grass and his presence beside her in the dimming twilight. Moments passed, maybe hours and days, she had no idea. He took a stone from the shore and threw it. It skimmed across the water, leaving spreading, rippling circles on the silvery surface, now tinted red from the setting sun over the trees in the distance. Three more stones followed the first one. Then quiet fell over the lake, as soft as a baby's sigh during sleep.

Jonah threw one more stone. Instead of skipping,

this one broke apart and sank. "Huh," he said. "I chose the wrong one."

Clara wanted to scream the same thing about Vernon, but like she had been telling herself, she had to be a good Beachy Amish woman and do the right thing for John and Edna.

Jonah turned from the lake to face her. The dimming sunlight, red as blood, stained one side of his face. "Do you ever feel like one of those stones?"

She didn't face him. "How do you mean?"

"Like life is a lake and you're sinking in it instead of skimming across it."

Clara knew what he meant. Except for happy moments here and there, she had felt like she was sinking in life ever since Abram had died. No, that wasn't right. She felt uplifted when she prayed. Her turmoil might bog her down from time to time, but God always sent a ray of sunshine to lift her from the storm. What bothered her about Jonah more than anything was how it seemed God had sent him to her and the children at exactly the time they needed him most. If that were true, why couldn't they be together as a family? Was she undergoing a trial of her faith to overcome temptation? She could see that, but something in her cut like a knife through her soul when she thought about marrying someone other than Jonah.

He picked up another stone and held it to the

dying light. "I thought this was an arrowhead, but it's just a piece of quartz. See how the light shines through it?"

Clara looked into the stone, similar to a piece of glass. "It's cracked."

Jonah lowered the stone. "It's a flaw." He offered it to her. "But I'll treasure it anyway if you'll keep it for me. I'm sure it's hard being Beachy Amish. You're expected to be perfect, but like us English, you're flawed like this stone. All you can do is try, then ask for forgiveness when you fail. That's all any of us can do."

Clara dropped the stone in her pocket. She had learned another side of Jonah: wisdom. Taking a deep breath, she smiled up at him. "You're right, that's all we can do. I'm going to bed, are you?"

"I'll sit on the deck a while. Sleep well."

Done in the bathroom, Clara lay in bed with the nightstand lamp on. In the bunk beds, John and Edna slept the sleep of innocent children. Shame burned through her. How could she have such deep feelings for Jonah? Not only was he English, he might not be Lydia's brother, and she might be his fiancé instead. Confusion joined the shame, until she turned off the lamp and prayed for clarity of thought as well as for forgiveness.

As drowsiness enclosed her like Abram's warm

hand enclosed hers in winter, peace washed over her. She would enjoy this week away from the toil at home, would enjoy the children and their simple play, would even enjoy Jonah and Lydia's relationship, whatever it was. After all, God expected her to care for everyone the same, and that's what she would do.

Chapter 4

Standing at the sliding glass doors, Clara listened to the patter of rain striking the wooden deck and spreading a gray curtain across the lake. Although she enjoyed the sound and the watery aroma, both were getting monotonous. To everyone's disappointment, a slight shower on the first night of their stay had turned into steady showers since Saturday, lasting four days so far. Not caring to turn the TV on, Jonah had checked the weather on his smart phone on Monday. If the forecast held true, the skies would clear tonight, and they would have at least two clear days before they had to leave Saturday.

On the sofa, Lydia was curled up with an Amish romance novel, surprising Clara. She didn't think Lydia was the type to read that kind of novel. In the easy chair near her end of the sofa, Jonah was reading the Bible. This didn't surprise Clara, since he had mentioned wanting to learn more of it.

She crossed her arms. John and Edna, having put all the cabin's puzzles together, plus being tired from staying up later than normal from doing it, were napping in Clara's big bed. If she had thought about it, she would've put them in the bunk beds and taken a nap in her bed. Now she was left to watch the rain and cover a yawn now and again.

Shoes thudded on the steps leading to the front door. Both Jonah and Lydia looked toward it. Someone knocked. Everyone looked at each other, eyebrows raising. Jonah got up and opened the door. "Can I help you?"

Clara couldn't see the person. "You can let us in before we drown," a woman's voice said.

Jonah stood aside as a woman and a man entered, both with closed umbrellas, dark with rain. They must've shaken them beneath the porch; neither dripped on the wooden floor.

The woman was as petite as Clara. She even had red hair like hers, except she wore it in a ponytail. Like Clara too, her eyes were an inquisitive and brilliant green. The man was tall and slender. His arms were wiry, as if he might've paddled a canoe on the lake like some people did before the rain came. He ran a hand through his dark brown hair. "We're sorry to bother y'all," he said, his voice a soft southern drawl. "We've put all our puzzles together and were wondering if y'all would like to trade."

"That's what we get for renting the cabin next

door without checking the weather forecast," the woman said. She flipped her hand in a friendly wave. "I'm Tess and this is Denver."

As Jonah introduced everyone, Clara noticed an engagement ring on Tess's ring finger but no wedding band. Maybe Denver was getting the milk without buying the cow like the English said. She clenched her teeth. Judging others was wrong. She would have to pray for forgiveness before bed.

Lydia moved to another chair and offered Denver and Tess the sofa. They leaned their umbrellas beside the door, and Jonah closed it . "I see your ring, Tess. Should we congratulate you and your fiancé?"

With a slight grin, Denver cut his eyes at Tess. "We're not engaged. We're just best friends."

Tess popped his hand. *"Just?* Is that all you think of me? We're more than best friends and you know it. After all, we have two children together."

Jonah's mouth fell open. "You're Denver Andrews, Eliza Andrews' husband."

"I thought I recognized you," Lydia said. "We saw you and Eliza at an art show in town last year."

Clara knew she shouldn't be so curious, but she couldn't help it. "A friend and I were selling tomatoes and baskets last year in town, and your wife bought some. After she left, my friend said you and your wife have a family. Do you mind if I ask—"

Denver laughed. "For an Amish woman, you sure are nosy."

Clara's cheeks warmed. "I'm sorry. I just—"

Denver held up his hand, stopping her. "I'm just teasing." He faced Tess. "Do you want to explain it? It's not like we haven't before."

"It's a long story," she said, facing Clara. "Did your friend tell you how Eliza used to be Amish?"

"She did. She said her family left the Amish to move here to be near her and Denver."

"That's right, and I'm Eliza's sister. She and Denver lost their first baby, and it almost destroyed their marriage. She even left him to teach sign language back in Ohio, with my brother."

"That would've killed me if it hadn't been for Tess," Denver said. "I was a mess, drinking too much and being depressed. One thing led to another, and Tess and I fell in love."

Lydia held up the Amish novel. "You should have someone write your story. It sounds like a soap opera."

"That's kind of how it was," Denver said. "Anyway, Tess knew Eliza and I belonged together, so she made it happen."

Jonah shook his head. "I don't get it. How can you and Tess have kids and you're still married to

Eliza?"

"And how can she let you stay in a cabin together?" Lydia asked.

"Are you engaged to someone else?" Clara asked Tess. "That could mean you're best friends like you said."

Tess raised her left hand and wiggled her fingers. "Nope. Denver gave me this. He told you we were engaged."

Blinking and shaking her head, Lydia worked her mouth like she was a fish out of water. "Are you sure you were Amish? Maybe you were Mormon. Don't they have more than one wife?"

Tess burst out laughing. Watching her, Denver chuckled, then faced Clara. "Being Amish, I'm sure this is confusing. Do you know what a sperm donor is?"

Clara had never heard of such a thing. "Should I?"

Lydia came over and whispered in her ear. "That's what it is."

Jonah laughed. "Don't let your face catch on fire, Clara. It's as red as your hair."

Clara touched her cheeks. She had never been so embarrassed. "I still don't understand how you're here alone together. Isn't your wife jealous?"

"Well," Tess said, "let me explain about our

children. After I helped Denver and Eliza get back together, I wanted a family too, so I went to a clinic and chose donors for them. You see, Eliza was helping an Amish family in Ohio. The woman was deaf and was hit by one of those big milk tankers. Her husband had cancer. They both died on the same day. They didn't have any family, so they wanted Eliza to adopt their son. He's as sweet as can be."

"He sure is," Denver said. "He loves fishing and water skiing."

"Anyway," Tess said, "since Denver adopted David—he's that couple's son—Eliza understood when I asked her if he could adopt my kids, so now they're our kids."

"And we *are* best friends," Denver said, "but we're closer than most best friends. We like to get away once in a while and talk about all our kids and just catch up. Tess and I build guitars together. Although we see each other most every day, it isn't the same. And," he added, "there's nothing physical going on between us, as hard as it might be to believe. "I'm as devoted to Eliza as she is to me."

"And I'm devoted to them both," Tess said, "or I wouldn't have helped them get back together. Our family and our close friends understand, so that's a plus."

"There was that reporter at the art show in Raleigh one time," Denver said. "He was nice at first, asking us about our family dynamics. Then he insulted Tess by asking if she thought she was manipulative and selfish by expecting me to adopt her children."

"I don't understand," Clara said to Tess. "Why would a reporter think that if you told Denver about adopting your kids before you had them."

"Because I didn't tell him before I had the first one. I did tell Eliza and my mama and papa. Like I said a minute ago, since Eliza asked Denver to adopt David, she understood. Mama and Papa moved here to be near the grandchildren they knew Eliza and Denver would have, so they understood too."

"How did the reporter know all that?" Lydia asked.

"You know reporters," Denver said. "A lot of them are always looking for some sensational headline to create gossip. To head that off, Tess, Eliza, and I granted an interview to our pastor, and we put it on Eliza's website."

Clara marveled at their story. This was one of the most understanding families she had ever heard of, filled with love and acceptance of each other, despite many issues that could've created hard feelings.

Jonah offered them coffee, but Denver and Tess stood, saying they had a pot going now. He checked his watch. "It's getting late. Let's run to town for supper at the brewery. We'll pick up some puzzles after."

"Good idea," Tess said. "I'll call Eliza to come eat with is. Mama and Papa will be glad to keep the kids."

Denver turned. "It was nice to meet y'all. We didn't mean to tell our story, but we don't mind."

After they left, Lydia went to the kitchen and threw the novel in the trash, then came back to flop down on the sofa. "I've heard it all now. My book will bore me to tears after listening to that."

Nodding in agreement, Jonah picked up his Bible and opened it.

Although Clara was inclined to agree with Lydia's statement, she thought the love within Denver and Eliza's family must be remarkable. Few families would make those allowances, especially an Amish family. She could understand that too. The Amish got their direction and faith from the Bible, but then Denver had mentioned their pastor, so he must've accepted their story too. After all, since Denver and Tess weren't having a physical relationship, there was no sin in the relationship, and his willingness to adopt the son of the couple who died, and Tess's kids, meant he loved them as if they were his own.

Clara left the chair she had taken during the conversation. At the sliding glass doors, she wrapped her arms around herself, recreating how Abram used to hold her while they watched the rain. She had once thought of Noah as a husband. Last year, when Jonah had driven her and the children to Pennsylvania to visit both sets of grandparents, she had gone to see Noah at his house through the woods, behind her parent's house. Upon seeing him, old feelings resurfaced, soon replaced by resentment at his teasing ways. She had forgotten those ways, which is why she had grown impatient with him and left after a short while. Before she met Abram at a local church sing, she never gave another young man other than Noah a thought. He was her world, his smile, his laugh, the way he bashfully slipped his hand into hers the one time he walked her home after another singing. Maybe she shouldn't have dismissed his idea of courting him instead of Vernon so quickly when they met again last year. With their past to draw them together, love stood a better chance between them than between her and Vernon.

Curled up on the sofa again, Lydia was propping her elbow on the back of it with her head in her hand and her eyes closed. Her head slipped off, and her eyes blinked sleepily. "If it weren't so late, Clara, I'd take you to my favorite clothing store in town."

"Why's it your favorite?" Clara asked.

"You'll see when we go tomorrow."

"It's a good thing we already got shorts and T-shirts for John and Edna," Jonah said. "I can take them swimming while y'all shop."

Clara didn't mind that. She didn't care to go to a swimming area filled with people wearing skimpy bathing suits while her long, blue dress and white kapp drew curious stares. Thankfully, the children would be more concerned with playing in the water than anyone looking at them. She wondered if Jonah would ogle the women, or if he had the discipline to keep his eyes down like Beachy Amish men did. Then again, last year, when he and Lydia had taken her, the children, and Vernon fishing on a pontoon boat, Vernon had ogled a scantily clad young woman water skiing.

Still watching the rain, Clara crossed her arms. *Men.*

Chapter 5

Standing on the sidewalk outside the clothing store called Hite's, Clara waved to John and Edna as Jonah drove his pickup away. They were going to the swimming area he had mentioned, and all three wore shorts, T-shirts, and plenty of sunscreen. Beside Clara, Lydia waved too. "John and Edna sure bring out the kid in Jonah. He's as excited to take them swimming as they are to go." She turned and gestured toward the store. "Hite's has a men's section on the left and a women's section on the right, sort of like how the men and women sit on different sides during Amish church services."

"We don't do that," Clara said, wondering how Lydia knew about the seating arrangements in many Amish churches. "We voted on it as a community and decided against it," she explained. "Besides, we meet in homes, not a building with pews. We hope to build a church when our community grows larger. It only started five years ago." She further explained how they should have two ministers, plus how a Beachy Amish Mennonite community would normally not socially interact with English like she was doing, but her community had voted to do so in order to set an example of Christian doctrine for anyone who might ask.

Lydia pointed at a store to the right of Hite's. "That's the Cottage Barn. They have the best bar-b-que sandwiches and ice cream. Maybe we'll get a bite there after we shop for clothes."

Puzzled as to what she might buy in a clothing store for English women, Clara followed Lydia into the women's side of the store. At a counter farther along, a woman with blonde hair waved. "Hey, Lydia. You're back already, huh?"

"I sure am." Lydia went to the counter. Clara hurried after her, her dress swishing against her legs. "This is my neighbor, Clara," Lydia said. "Isn't she pretty? I'm hoping I can tempt her into trying on some of your dresses." Lydia cast a sidelong glance at Clara. "And maybe some naughty clothes too, if you know what I mean."

The woman shook her head. "Don't you listen to Lydia, Clara. She may like to tease, but she has a good eye for clothes."

"Not as good as you," Lydia said. "I see you in your Facebook ads. You always look so nice."

Waving the remark away, the woman faced

Clara. "I'm Ren. Lydia's right, you *are* pretty."

"How about those green eyes?" Lydia asked.

"I agree," Ren said. "She reminds me of a cat about to pounce on a—"

"On a man?" Lydia said, grinning suggestively.

Clara's cheeks warmed. She shouldn't have come into the store. "I'm sorry, I should go."

Lydia looped her arm within Clara's. "I'm just teasing. Let's see what we can find."

Ren led them to a rack of flowing, knee-length dresses. Although Clara understood why the women in her community wore simple dresses to emphasize modesty, the colors and patterns intrigued her, especially the floral patterns. She ran her fingertips along the collar of one dress. Unlike her dress, the cloth felt smooth and soft.

"Do you like that one?" Ren asked.

Clara pulled her hand back as if she had been burned. "It's beautiful."

"The green in it would show off your red hair." Ren shared a soft smile with Clara. "I realize you have certain rules about your clothes, but if you'd like to try it on just to see how it looks, you can."

Pretending to admire another dress, Clara turned away. *Please, God, strengthen me against these temptations. My woman's heart wants so much to try on that dress, but I know it's wrong.*

A gentle hand touched her shoulder, and Ren looked into Clara's eyes. "I enjoy selling clothes to ladies for a lot of reasons. Deep down, we know our beauty comes from the inside, but sometimes we like seeing ourselves in a new dress, or a new blouse. I look at it like the flowers in spring—they get to try on new clothes too, even if it's only once a year. You don't have to try it on, but it would make my day to see you in it."

"I …" Clara hesitated. Would it be so wrong to simply try a dress on? "Can I stay in the dressing room?"

"No way," Lydia said. "You need to let the world see how pretty you are."

"You can do whatever you like," Ren said.

Clara nodded, still unsure. Ren checked the dress's tag, chose another size, and led Clara to the dressing room. Inside, she quickly removed her kapp so the sky-blue dress wouldn't hang on it. As she lowered the floral dress over her shoulders, her hair came loose from the pins, releasing a flowing waterfall of red along her shoulders and down her back.

Someone knocked on the door. "It's Lydia. Open up so I can give you something." Clara opened the door slightly. Lydia gave her a pair of high-heeled sandals in green leather. "Hey, if you're gonna dress up, you might as well do it right."

Clara zipped the dress and leaned against a wall to put on the sandals. Looking in the mirror, she didn't even recognize herself. She felt transformed, exactly like a flower blooming in the springtime as Ren had said.

"Can we see?" Ren asked.

Feeling a bit embarrassed, Clara opened the door. "Oh, my," Ren said. "You could be a fashion model on a magazine cover."

"She sure could," Lydia said. "But a shorter one." In her purse, her cell phone rang. "I bet that's Jonah." Stepping away, she answered the phone.

"Turn around and let me get a look at you, okay?" Ren asked. Clara did so, loving the silky feel of the soft fabric against her legs.

Lydia put the phone away. "Jonah says the kids are having a blast."

Ren tilted her head toward the men's section. "I think you have an audience.

By a table of Lake Country T-shirts, three young men were staring at Clara. One of the men's mouths was hanging open.

"How do you know they aren't looking at me?" Lydia asked.

"I'm sure they're looking at both of you," Ren said.

But they're not looking at us like we're flowers, Clara

thought. She closed the dressing room door and snatched the sinful dress off, pinned her hair back up and put on her kapp, then put her tennis shoes back on and came out to give Ren the dress and sandals. "Thank you for letting me try everything on. It made me feel wonderful until those men looked at me like that. That's one of the reasons our Ordnung says we should wear plain clothes."

Ren left to tend to a customer. Lydia came over with another dress. The shimmering green, as deeply colored as the foliage on the trees in summer, caught Clara's eye, as well as the extremely short length. "This is silk," Lydia said. "I bet Vernon would like it for your first night together when you get married."

If we get married, Clara thought. She couldn't see wearing this dress for Vernon, but as attractive as it made her feel, she could see wearing it for Jonah, or maybe Noah.

Lydia held the dress to her shoulders. "It's okay, but I'd like something skimpier when I get married."

Clara had never heard that word. "What do you mean by 'skimpier?'"

Pursing her lips into a grin, Lydia shoved Clara's shoulder. "I mean something that's next to nothing. You know, to drive a man wild in bed."

Clara ignored the last part. Now that she knew

what that word meant, something else bothered her. The way Lydia said "when I get married" sounded like she meant sometime soon, and the only person Clara knew who might marry her was Jonah, if they weren't brother and sister.

Lydia went to another rack of skimpy clothes. In the opening between the men's section and the women's section, a tall man with broad shoulders walked by, facing away from Clara. He wore a wide-brimmed hat like Noah was wearing in his garden. She raised her hand to her mouth. Like a butterfly nearing a flower, her heart fluttered in her chest. Although the man couldn't be Noah, Clara wished he was. Not only would he get her mind off of courting Vernon soon, like she had promised, he would get her mind off of her feelings for Jonah.

The man went beyond the opening. While Lydia continued looking at clothes, Clara looked at shoes. She could use a sturdy pair of leather boots for winter, coming in only a few months. As she studied a pair, more stylish than work boots, she saw the sandals Lydia had made her try on, where Ren had returned them. Before the children came along, after a long day of work on the farm, Abram used to have Clara sit on the bed and place her feet in his lap so he could massage them.

Like with not seeing herself wearing that silk

dress for Vernon, she couldn't see him massaging her feet like Abram used to do.

Lydia came over, a bag in her hand. "Aw, go on and buy those sandals. Your tiny feet looked so sexy in them."

Clara picked a pair of the leather boots, then the sandals. They were shoes, after all, and they would be cool during the remaining days of summer. Being high heels, they would help her reach things on the top shelves in the kitchen cabinets.

At the counter, after Clara put the change in her leather clutch and returned it to her dress pocket, Ren thanked her for the purchases, remarking how she enjoyed meeting her and to please come back any time, even if just to say hello. Lydia mentioned how they should visit the Woodbine Vineyard west of town, as some Old Order Amish drank wine in moderation. Clara said their community had voted against drinking alcohol. Ren said they could visit anyway, that they had a huge barn and other things to drink, plus live music at certain times and a lovely view of a farmhouse and a pond, with chairs beneath two huge oak trees for sitting in the shade. Clara agreed that it sounded lovely, and Lydia again said they would have to visit.

Outside the store, she checked her watch. "Let's go to the thrift store around the corner. Maybe you'll find something there you like. They mark the clothes half off sometimes. Jonah buys clothes there all the time, for his frugal self."

Beside Lydia, Clara realized another one of Jonah's qualities that matched the Beachy Amish: they chose to be frugal as well, preferring to purchase things they needed instead of things they wanted.

She and Lydia strolled the sidewalk between Hite's and a large bank building. Nearing the thrift store, Lydia stopped. "I forgot, today's Thursday. The store's only open on Fridays and Saturdays." She turned sharply and looped her arm within Clara's. "Let's have that bite to eat at the Cottage Barn."

In the store, they both ordered bar-b-que sandwiches with coleslaw and bottles of water and sat in a booth. Between bites of the savory sandwich, Lydia told Clara about the thrift store, run by the local Ruritan Club, which donated much of the proceeds to various charities. She also said the store hosted a band and dance on Friday nights. It sold furniture, kitchen items, used shoes, sewing supplies, sporting goods, and books. Clara was glad the store was closed. If many people were there, she might feel like the wrong baby bird in a nest, her blue dress and white kapp marking her as coming from a different egg altogether.

She drank a swallow of the cold water.

The clash of Amish and English sometimes twisted her thoughts into knots, such as her struggle with wearing a dress much like her own, but with a floral pattern that mimicked nature. No doubt Alison would love such a dress and those high-heeled sandals. She had even admitted to buying a lace bra and panties once to see Samuel's reaction. When Clara asked about it, her best friend had only grinned, then added that's how they had conceived their third son. Clara had also asked how wearing those things brought attention to her, which the Amish weren't supposed to do, which had brought a grinning frown from Alison, and a, "Why, Clara, I was just pretending to be dessert after supper. Don't you do the same for Abram?" Although Clara had agreed inwardly, she didn't care to discuss what went on in the marriage bed, not even with Alison. Then again, although some Amish doctrine judged physical intimacy for pleasure only—not the act of procreation—as something to be avoided, why couldn't two best friends discuss the intimacy between them and their husbands and how it deepened the bonds of marriage? After all, along with faith in God, marriage and families were the bedrock of the community, and with the increasing numbers of Amish leaving their orders for the English lifestyle, this might be reduced if they could be more open about subjects that could draw them together instead of driving them apart.

Clara was tempted to toss her hand in the air to dismiss her thoughts. She was just a woman. What did she know about anything? She should concentrate on faith, family, and community. If she did that, everything would work out.

Lydia finished her sandwich and bought them a serving each of butter pecan ice cream. Closing her eyes at the luscious combination of buttery and nutty flavor, Clara realized how much she was enjoying her outing. Still, she regretted how trying that dress on had made her feel. No, it wasn't that; it was how those young men had stared at her, as if their mouths were watering over a piece of apple pie steaming on a plate. That wasn't her fault at all, nor was it her fault that men, and even women, as Lydia had said, thought she was pretty. God knitted her together in the womb, every part of her touched with His gentle fingertip of love. She should be able to rejoice in gratitude of each and every aspect of how he had created her, not hide it away under a plain dress and a kapp.

Clara frowned. More blasphemy. More failure. More sin. At least she could enjoy the delicious ice cream without guilt, at least not any that she knew of.

Behind her, as she was sitting in the booth facing away from the door, its latch clicked, followed by heavy footsteps coming closer on the wooden floor. The same man Clara had seen in Hite's, wearing the wide-brimmed straw hat, tipped it at her and Lydia. "Good day, ladies." His focus left Lydia and returned to Clara. "Do you mind if I ask what community you belong to? I'm Mennonite myself. I live in Nathalie, in Halifax County."

"My community is north of there," she said. "We're Beachy Amish Mennonites." The man's resemblance to Noah shocked Clara. They could easily be twins.

"That ice cream looks good," he said. "I'll give it a try."

He did so, saying "Mmm," as he left the store.

Lydia's eyes followed him. "'Mmm' is right. What a beef steer *he* would make."

Clara couldn't disagree. Not only did the man make her think of Noah, he made her think of Jonah.

Lydia finished her ice cream and pushed the bowl aside on the table. "Clara, we've known each other for over a year now. I've seen you and Jonah together a lot, and I realize you're good friends, maybe even more than good friends. Am I wrong or right?"

Clara had to consciously keep her mouth from falling open at Lydia's question. "Why would you ask that when he's Eng—"

"I know, I know, he's English. I just don't want you to make a mistake by marrying Vernon. He's nice, but he's sort of a stuffed shirt. Then there's the rumor about his wife divorcing him. Is there anything to that?"

"It's just a rumor," Clara said, trying to keep the sharp tone of anger from her voice.

"Well, where there's smoke, there's fire." Lydia paused. "Did your community vote on whether or not it would allow a divorced person to marry? I don't know of any Ordnungs that do; their doctrine strictly forbids it."

Wondering again how Lydia knew so much about Amish and Mennonite doctrine, Clara looked away and back. "I never thought about it." Should she tell Lydia what Vernon had said about his wife dying? No, because it had no bearing on his asking Clara to court him. He was a fine man with a Godly heart. He would never lie about something so serious.

But an inkling of doubt crept into her mind. She faced Lydia. "Aside from Amish people not being able to divorce, how does it affect them if they do?"

Lydia rolled her eyes. "How can you not know

that? They can't remarry unless they leave their order. Then they're shunned." She shared a soft but smirking smile. "I'm sure your Vernon is an honorable man, but Jonah is *more* honorable. Are you sure you don't have feelings for him?"

Although Lydia's line of questioning suggested she was Jonah's sister, the way she sometimes glanced at him suggested otherwise. Then there was the issue of her crooked left arm, with a scar inside the elbow. If Clara didn't know any better, someone had grabbed her and broken her arm, resulting in surgery on the joint. Jonah, as gentle and kind as he was, would never do that. If that's what had happened, who *had* done that?

To give herself time to think, Clara threw her empty ice cream bowl away and returned to the booth. "Yes, I love Jonah like you do—as if he were my brother. Does that answer your question?"

Without any hint of a grin this time, Lydia smirked. "Liar." Then she grinned. "I'm just teasing." She took her cell phone from her jeans pocket. "Let me call Jonah to pick us up. We need to plan supper and John and Edna's birthday party tomorrow, or has our shopping trip made you forget about that?"

As Lydia swiped the screen, Clara got up to look at some of the hand-painted furniture in the store, or rather, she pretended to look at it. Yes, it was very nice, but all she could think about was how she had forgotten her plans to combine John and Edna's birthday party on this camping trip. She hadn't really thought about what to do. Maybe Jonah, as good as he was with the children, would suggest something. First, she needed to get back to the cabin and away from Lydia for some quiet time to pray about this confusing day.

Chapter 6

As soon as Lydia closed the pickup door, John and Edna excitedly told Clara how Jonah had taught them to float on their backs. Their cheeks were kissed golden by the sun, but Jonah's were red. "I was having so much fun with these two," he explained, "I forgot to put sunscreen on when I put it on them." Lydia said she had some cream that would help. Clara thanked Jonah for taking such good care of them, but added he needed to do the same for himself.

When they got to the cabin, Jonah stretched out on the sofa. "I'm worn out, and my sunburn is making me feel rough."

John and Edna tugged his hands. "We wanna do something," John whined.

"Let's go hiking," Edna said. "You said we could. You said there's a trail here."

"There's lots of trails here," Lydia said. "Did you have lunch, or do you want to wait until supper?"

"We got hot dogs at the store on this side of the bridge," Jonah said. He covered a yawn. "Y'all go hiking if you want. I'm staying right here in the air conditioning."

Lydia opened the door. "Do you want to come, Clara?"

Having had enough of Lydia this morning, Clara declined. "Go ahead. Just make sure to wear those two out so they sleep well tonight." Clara paused. Neither John nor Edna had mentioned their combined birthday party. She would ask Jonah about something to do while they were hiking, and it would be a surprise.

Lydia closed the door behind them. Clara sat in the chair across from Jonah. "What can we do for their birthdays? I almost forgot."

Touching one cheek, Jonah winced. "Can you check the bathroom? Lydia's makeup is in there. That cream might be with it."

Clara found the cream and returned to give it to him. In the chair again, she waited for him to apply the cream, but he just held the jar and closed his eyes. "What if we go out to eat for their birthday? The Bridgewater in town is nice. We'll do it tomorrow night. We have to leave Saturday, and I'm too tired to go tonight."

Clara agreed with his plan. She hadn't eaten out in a nice restaurant since the weekend after she and Abram were married, when family visits had dwindled, so the change would be interesting.

Yawning like Jonah, she took the shoes she had bought from Hite's to her bedroom and came back to the chair. A softly snoring Jonah startled awake at the sound of her footsteps. He shoved the jar at her. "Can you put this stuff on my cheeks. I don't feel like getting up and looking in a mirror."

Clara refused the jar. Rubbing his cheeks would be entirely too personal. She returned to the chair, and Jonah eyed her. "I can't believe you'll ignore your best friend, especially when his face feels like it's been in an oven all day." He got up and knelt at her feet. "I'll even take your shoes off so you can kneel beside the sofa and be comfortable."

Before Clara could jerk her feet back, he grabbed both feet, pulled her tennis shoes off, and waved a hand in front of his nose. "Whew-wee, and I thought my feet smelled."

Clara kicked him away, and he fell on his rear end. "My feet smell because I'm not wearing socks and they sweated," she said. "What excuse do you have?"

He sat up again. "Do Beachy Amish Mennonites wash each other's feet like the Mennonites do?"

To Clara, Jonah and Lydia knew more about the Amish and the Mennonites than most people. Maybe they just read a lot. After all, they had a computer in their house. "Our community doesn't do that, why?"

"I thought I could wash your feet before the smell takes the finish off the wood floor. I'd hate to get charged for damage to the cabin."

Pursing her lips together tightly, Clara tried not to laugh.

"Go ahead," Jonah said. "You know you want to." He grabbed her feet again and tickled them, and it was all she could to not scream. He stopped. "Okay, no more tickling if you help me with my face." He returned to the sofa and offered her the jar. "Please?"

Like lightning arcing from cloud to cloud during a summer storm, the heat of conflict arced through Clara's mind. At least putting the cream on his cheeks would be less intimate than him washing her feet, so similar to Abram massaging them. She knelt by the sofa and opened the jar. "Close your eyes, you big baby. I don't want any to get in them." He did. Clara dabbed the cream on the cheek facing her and gently spread it around. His tiny dark whiskers felt like sandpaper beneath her fingertips. His nostrils flared with his breaths. She noticed the hint of a cleft in his chin. With her fingertips, she eased his face over so she could get to his other cheek.

"Mmm," he moaned. "That feels better already, Clara." She capped the jar and set it on the table at the end of the sofa. He opened his eyes and smiled. "Look at you, your hair's coming loose from the pins."

For a moment, Clara expected him to look at her like the men at the store had, but she knew better. Jonah was different in every way from men like them. Regardless, as she started to tuck the loose strands under the kapp, he took her wrist in his large hand. He didn't squeeze it; he just pulled her hand away from her hair. "Your hair was braided that night we took a drive in Pennsylvania. Can I see it down?"

Clara's heart exploded with confusion. Was he like those men after all, only looking at her with hunger in their eyes? She needed to know, needed to be sure. If he were like those men, it would be much easier to stop thinking of him as someone she cared about so much. She removed the kapp and the pins. Her hair flowed across her shoulders and down to her waist.

He smiled again, softer this time, just a hint, just the smallest hint. His hand raised. Its palm cupped her cheek. "Did you know I think of you as my angel?"

Clara didn't know how to answer, so she didn't. The warmth of his palm spread to her ear, down her neck, across her shoulders. One breath, two breaths, three. "Why do you think of me that way,

Jonah?"

"Before I met you, I was going through some things. They're not important now."

"What things? Can't I know? We're best friends, remember? Best friends tell each other everything, especially when it's bothering them."

"It stopped bothering me when we admitted to having feelings for each other last year. When we did that, I realized my problems weren't problems after all." His thumb traced a circle on the skin below her eye. "You're a wonderful woman in every way. You're intelligent. You learned how to drive your pickup and transferred that knowledge to the tractor. You're kind and sweet, and John and Edna couldn't have a better mother. You fill my soul every time I look at you. Don't you understand what I'm trying to say?"

The sting of tears threatened behind Clara's eyes. She knew exactly what he was trying to say. *God forgive me*, she prayed. *I need this wonderful man in my life, and the only way I can do that is to leave my community.* Smiling, she nodded. "I know what you're trying to say. I love you too."

"I know," he said. "Best friends love each other, and you're my best friend. I'll always need you in my life, even if I get married." He laughed. "And my wife will either have to accept that or find someone else."

Clara's heart, which was exploding with love instead of confusion, imploded with an agony that threatened to engulf her from head to toe. He didn't love her like she loved him. In fact, he didn't even have feelings for he like he had admitted last year. Her threatening tears turned to ice. She stood, glad he had explained his feelings toward her. Now she could concentrate on courting Vernon. The children needed a father and she needed a husband. She was tired of working all the time anyway. The husbands in their community had their work to do and the wives had theirs."

She returned the jar to the bathroom. In her bedroom, she pinned her hair back up and covered it with the kapp. She hadn't brought her phone because Vernon had said he would be too busy to call during his trip. If she had, she would've called him now and told him they could start courting. Regardless of this decision, she cringed at the idea. She would have to pray about it at bedtime tonight. Once her soul was settled, she could set her mind on John and Edna's birthday party tomorrow night at that restaurant Jonah had mentioned. Then she could go back home with a clear conscious and her faith restored, with how she was doing the right thing for the children and for her community by considering Vernon as a husband.

She went back to the living room to ask Jonah what time they were leaving for home Saturday, but he was softly snoring. How could she have been so stupid to think she could love someone outside of the Beachy Amish Mennonite order? Hadn't the shopping trip into town with Lydia shown her how the English ignored the common decency of not staring at a woman who was simply trying on a dress?

In her room again, she sat on the bed to pray. On the nightstand, beside the lamp, the quartz stone Jonah had asked her to keep reminded her how he wasn't like those men in town. He really was her best friend. Time and time again he had helped her with so many things. Saving Edna's life when a Black Widow spider bit her was the most important, but he had plowed the garden and helped her plant it last spring too. Then, when Clara had miscarried in the hospital, he had insisted she and the children stay with him and Lydia until she could take care of herself and them at home.

Clara pursed her lips. The mystery of who had given her the propane stove last year had never been solved. Jonah and Vernon both denied knowing anything about it, so she had decided to accept it as a blessing from God, one that didn't need wood to cook with. Along with those occurrences, there was the issue of someone setting up what a nurse had called a "Go Fund Me Account" to pay Clara and Edna's hospital bills. Like with the propane stove, that was a mystery too.

The curtains were drawn and the room was shadowed. Clara turned on the lamp. The quartz stone glittered in the light.

Jonah had called her his angel because she had somehow helped him through whatever things he was going through when they met.

She picked up the stone, tempted to take it back to the shore of the lake where he had given it to her. It belonged there like she belonged with the Beachy Amish and he belonged with the English. If God, in His strength and mercy, would help her, she would never consider Jonah anything but a friend from this day on.

Isaiah 40:29 came to mind. She had prayed it over and over in the days and nights following Abram's death.

"He gives power to the weak and strength to the powerless," she whispered, hoping the words would lift up to the Heavens. Instead, she felt as if they had never left her lips. Whenever she looked into Jonah's brown eyes and thought about how he had held her in his lap in his pickup in

Pennsylvania to comfort her on that night so long ago, she became powerless to deny her feelings for him.

She took her leather clutch from her pocket and put the stone in it. The day she had to give up on the hope of her and Jonah being together, she would drive here and throw it in the lake. Until then, she would shove that hope aside and give Vernon a fair chance during their courtship.

Chapter 7

At the end of the bridge entering Clarksville, Clara peered up at the sign as Jonah drove by. "You didn't say this restaurant has a bar, Jonah. I'm not sure if I want myself or the children to be around drunkards."

Chuckling, he turned into the parking lot. "Well, well. Aren't you the judgmental sort?"

"It's not judgmental. I don't want the children to see that kind of thing."

"Don't worry," Lydia said from the front passenger seat. "No one will be drunk here. If anyone is drinking, it's just to be sociable."

"What's wrong with talking to be sociable?" Clara asked, feeling her cheeks getting red with anger.

"Nothing," Jonah said. He parked and turned around to face Clara. "I understand how you feel. Lydia and I rarely drink, but there's a difference between drinking and a drunkard. Have you ever read—"

"Yes, Jonah, I've read plenty of Bible verses about drinking in moderation." Clara paused. She had spoken with contempt in her voice, and she didn't like doing it. "I'm sorry for my tone, but I've heard of men in some Beachy Amish communities mistreating their families because of strong drink."

"And drugs," Lydia said. "I admire a lot about the Amish and Mennonites, but they're human like anyone else. Like anyone else, they can and do fail. Not all of them, of course, but some of them."

Clara said nothing. Like she had failed with her attraction to Jonah.

Everyone climbed from the pickup. In the restaurant, Jonah told the greeter he had a reservation. Her gaze drifted over Clara and the children, no doubt at Clara and Edna's blue dresses and white kapps and John's dark pants supported with black suspenders over a white shirt. Like a little gentleman, he removed his wide-brimmed straw hat and smiled at the greeter. "I'm John." He took Edna's hand. "This is my sister, Edna. "It's our birthday."

Clara explained how they were celebrating their birthdays together. "How sweet," the young woman said. She led everyone past several booths and tables, past an open partition to a back room, where she gestured to a large table. "Here you go. Someone will take your drink orders in a minute."

From around the partition, Denver and Eliza

Andrews appeared. "I thought that was you," he said. "Eliza and I were in a booth in the bar when I saw you walk by."

Jonah stood and shook Denver's hand. "Hey, Denver, it's good to see you." He offered his hand to Eliza, lovely in a gray dress that enhanced her dark eyes and black hair that fell past her shoulders. "I'm Jonah. We enjoyed meeting Denver and Tess at the park the other day. It's obvious y'all have a special relationship."

Denver laughed. "So special she's keeping the kids to give me and Eliza a night alone."

"Phooey," Lydia said. "I was hoping you could join us."

Denver and Eliza sat, thanking Lydia for the invitation. A waitress took their drink orders. Denver ordered a beer. Eliza ordered a glass of wine. Clara asked God to forgive her for being judgmental, but she didn't care for alcohol, much less someone drinking it at the same table where John and Edna were.

The drinks arrived. About to sip wine, Eliza lowered the glass and faced Clara. Being Amish, I hope you don't mind us drinking."

"They're Beachy Amish Mennonite," Jonah said. "Their Ordnung even allows most every technology, except TV and radio."

Clara sipped sweet tea with lemon. "If you don't

mind me saying, I don't think I could allow my husband to stay in a cabin with my sister, especially as attractive as she is."

"She sure is," Jonah said.

Denver eyed Clara, then faced Eliza. "I explained everything. Maybe Clara didn't understand."

"Well," Eliza said, "it *is* complicated."

"It isn't to me," Lydia said, cutting her eyes at Clara. "I'm not judgmental like some people. It's about a family accepting a certain kind of love, that's all."

Drinking beer, Denver lowered his glass. "Exactly. If it weren't for Tess's love for us, Eliza and I wouldn't be together."

Shame crept into Clara's heart, but not enough shame to stop her from asking another question. "Does Tess date other men?" She glanced at Jonah. "Since someone thinks she's so attractive, maybe someone should ask her out."

"She does from time to time," Eliza said. She faced Jonah. "When she and Denver told me about seeing you at the park, she said you were cute. Do you want me to ask her?"

Lydia and Clara's mouths fell open, and Jonah laughed. "Thanks, but between work and my farm, I don't have time for romance." He paused.

"Denver, you said you and Tess build guitars. Do you both play?"

"I tried years ago but gave it up. She plays really well, why?"

"I was thinking about giving it a shot."

Denver took a card from his wallet and gave it to Jonah. "Call her and see. If you need a guitar, she makes a low-cost model for beginners. I'm sure she'd love to spend some time with you."

Trying not to purse her lips, Clara had no doubt of Tess's desire to spend time with Jonah, as well as his desire to spend time with the attractive Tess.

The waitress returned with their food. John loved the fish tacos, saying he wanted Jonah to take them fishing again so Clara could make them. Shaking her head, Edna swallowed a bite of her chicken BLT. "No, John. I want Mama to make this sandwich. It's really good."

Clara swallowed a piece of chicken from her fried chicken salad. "I can buy fish at the grocery. We don't need to bother Jonah." Although she was enjoying the meal, Jonah's comment about them being friends after she had admitted her love for him still stung.

He swallowed a bite of ribeye steak. "It's no bother, Clara."

"I agree," Lydia said. "You two should spend more time together."

Like always, whenever Lydia commented about Clara and Jonah, it created confusion. It was almost as if she suspected something between them.

Denver sipped beer. "I had to get a larger pontoon boat for the family. With my in-laws and all the kids, we've got a boatload as it is."

Eliza kissed his cheek. "I'm glad we kept the old pontoon boat." She faced Clara. "That's where my husband finally fell in love with me." She paused. "He didn't mention it when he told me about meeting you at the park, but I see your husband isn't here. Do you mind if I ask why?"

Drinking sweet tea, Edna lowered her glass. "Papa fell out of the barn and went to Heaven."

John nodded. "He's an angel."

Blinking furiously, Eliza wiped tears with a napkin. "I'm so sorry," she said to Clara. "I wouldn't have asked if I had known." She put the napkin down. "Except for Denver, my papa is the most important man in my life. I couldn't imagine losing him. If it weren't for him, I wouldn't have met Denver."

Denver explained how he met Eliza in Ohio, when he went there to teach sign language, then how she went on to become a famous artist. The story amazed Clara. Not only had Eliza fallen in love with an outsider, her family had left the strictest Amish order—the Swartzentruber Amish—to be with her and Denver in Clarksville. Yes, love came in all forms, and it had certainly found its way into this remarkable family. The thought both saddened and uplifted Clara. If Eliza and Denver could conquer so many barriers to find love together, maybe she and Jonah could conquer their own barriers.

The waitress returned with two others. They sang Happy Birthday to a grinning Edna and John. Denver suggested banana pudding for dessert.

"Nanners in puddin'?" John asked, frowning at Clara.

"Our son David loves it," Eliza said. "He called it 'nanner puddin' when he was younger too."

Everyone ordered the banana pudding. Between bites, Jonah told Denver about his beef cattle herd. Lydia and Eliza talked about how they loved shopping in Clarksville.

After a bite of banana pudding, Eliza faced Clara. "I bought tomatoes from you last year at your stand in town. They were delicious."

Clara swallowed pudding. "I was with my friend Alison. We keep saying we'll come back but haven't yet."

When all the pudding was gone, Denver stood. The waitress had left separate tickets. He went around the table picking them up. "The birthday supper is on me. I enjoyed seeing y'all again."

"And I enjoyed meeting you," Eliza said. She faced Clara. "You have a lovely family." She glanced at Jonah and returned to Clara. "If you hope to marry again one day, I hope you find the right man. I know the Amish tend to think marriage is more about strengthening the community, but love is important too." She smiled at Denver. "And we're glad we never gave up on it. Goodnight."

"They were nice," Lydia said, facing Clara. "You could take a lesson. It's not nice to ask strangers personal questions like you asked about Denver staying in the cabin with Tess."

Jonah's eyes darted between Lydia and Clara, and she could see his displeasure with her. Who was he to judge her, keeping secrets about his and Lydia's relationship? She stood. "I'll have to send Denver a thank you card for John and Edna's birthday supper, won't I? Then you and Lydia can say I'm nice." Almost immediately, Clara regretted her icy tone.

Jonah took a pen and Tess's card from his pants pocket. Looking at the card, he wrote on the napkin, then put the pen and card away and gave the card to Clara. "There you go," he said sarcastically. "I'm sure Tess will get it to him."

* * *

After getting John and Edna into bed, Clara got ready in the bathroom. Down the hall, soft voices came from the living room: Jonah and Lydia talking about everything that had happened at the restaurant, no doubt.

Their voices quieted. Lydia's soft footsteps passed the bathroom door, but Jonah's didn't. Still wearing the blue dress, Clara padded barefoot to the living room, where Jonah was standing by the sliding glass doors, looking out at the lake. "I hear you," he said. "I'd know those bare feet anywhere."

Clara knew he meant the sound instead of the smell. If he weren't angry with her for how she had acted in the restaurant, he would've teased her about the smell. "Do you have Vernon's number in your phone? I left mine at home, and I'd like to call him."

"Why, to cry on his shoulder after acting like a child by judging people for daring to drink alcohol and having a different type of family than what you think they should?" He whirled to face Clara. "Making that comment about Denver and Tess was wrong and you know it. I can't imagine what he and Tess and Eliza went through, trying to pull their lives back together after he and Eliza lost their daughter. That Tess was willing to get them back together because she knew it was the right thing to do was amazing. I can only hope the woman I marry loves me as much as she loves him and Eliza."

A hot waterfall of emotions washed over Clara. Why couldn't Jonah see how much she loved him? That had to be why she had made those comments. She chewed her lower lip. No, she needed to forget her hopes about Jonah and call Vernon. Once she heard his voice, the comfort of doing the right thing would wash over her instead of the confusion she was now feeling. She held out her hand. "I just need the phone, not a sermon."

"A sermon?" He pulled the phone from his pocket and slapped it into her hand. "You must've forgotten all the sermons you've heard over the years. Does 'judge not, lest ye be judged' ring a bell? Or 'let he who is without sin cast the first stone?' I thought more of you, Clara. I guess I don't know you as well as I thought I did." He faced the door again. Beyond him, across the wide expanse of water, where moonlight reflected on a multitude of tiny waves, lights glowed in the windows of distant homes.

Denver said he had a pontoon boat. Some of those lights might be from his and Eliza's house—a house filled with family, a house filled with love.

The temptation to apologize raised Clara's hand to within an inch of Jonah's shoulder. His warmth seared her palm. How could he be so angry at her if they were best friends? He was supposed to try to understand her, wasn't he? His name trembled on her lips, but she was afraid to say it, afraid she had already lost him, even as a friend.

She lowered her hand and hurried to her room to sit on the bed. Maybe some Amish doctrine was right. They said to stay away from outsiders, to keep separate and shun their ways lest they corrupt them, like with strong drink and emotional weakness.

But was love an emotional weakness? It hadn't been with her and Abram. If anything, love had made their marriage stronger.

Clara resisted the urge to cry. She had choices to make, and she needed to make them now. The tone from Vernon's phone rang and rang. Even though she didn't have her phone, he could've called Jonah to speak with her if he had wanted to. She ended the call and tried again. Like before, it rang and rang, this time until it said his inbox was full.

Like a snake emerging from a hole, the suspicion about his wife divorcing him slithered from Clara's memory. Was he seeing her now, begging her to take him back? Was he such a liar as to make Clara believe he cared enough to court her? What about John and Edna? Would he let them think he cared about them until his wife took him back?

Clara had heard Jonah's heavy footsteps pass the bedroom door minutes ago. She took the phone to the kitchen and left it on the counter, where he would find it in the morning.

Crossing the living room on the way to the sliding glass doors, she shivered at the touch of the cold wooden floor. The doors slid open. The deck's wooden boards chilled her feet even more. A sudden breeze off the lake rustled her dress, blew the kapp off and freed her hair from the pins, resulting in a cascade of silky strands down her back and shoulders and along her bare arms.

From the far shore, maybe from where one of those lights glowed, the aroma of grilled food said someone was having a late supper—someone who was in love and happy, not confused and endlessly, hopelessly, sad.

Chapter 8

Saturday, after Jonah and Lydia dropped Clara and the children off at the house, Clara, glaring at the garden, placed her hands on her hips.

"It looks like a jungle in one of my books," Edna said from beside her.

John tugged Clara's dress. "Are we gonna plow it, Mama?"

Clara picked up the heavy suitcase, one Abram had bought in the event of them ever taking a honeymoon, which they never had. Even with the Beachy Amish custom of not taking a honeymoon, Clara thought it was a shame to not allow a couple to enjoy some place different for a few days after they were married, especially since the daily duties of working a farm would be there when they returned. "After I unpack," she said, lugging the suitcase toward the porch."

Edna opened the screen door. "Don't we have to wash clothes first? I need a clean dress for tomorrow."

"Me too," John said, nodding.

Edna giggled. "You mean pants, John."

He punched Edna's arm. "Don't laugh at me. That's mean."

She balled up her little fist and drew it back. Clara dropped the suitcase in the gravel driveway and grabbed Edna's arm before she could hit John. "No, ma'am," she said sharply. She released Edna's arm and waggled a finger at John. "And I mean you too, sir. We do not hit each other in this family, do you understand?"

"She laughed at me." John pushed his lips out in a pout.

"I saw you in my head wearing a dress," Edna said. "It was funny. What if I wore your pants? Wouldn't you laugh at me?"

"Your sister's right," Clara said. "Remember the Bible verse I taught you both about laughter being like a medicine? Besides, Edna wasn't laughing at you. She was laughing at the picture in her head."

John squinted up at her. "A Bible verse?"

Clara knelt beside her two precious children. No doubt they were tired from their long week away from home, which had led to their argument, so she would use this as a lesson, hopefully for life. She hugged them both at the same time, loving the sweet smell of baby shampoo in their hair, the fresh air in their clothes, the warmth of their small bodies held close, and released them. "You two are such a blessing to me and your papa."

"I miss him," Edna said, fingering a tear from the corner of one eye.

John gave her a squeeze. "Don't cry, Papa's in Heaven. He knows we're okay." He faced Clara, a question in his furrowed brow. "Can Jonah be our next papa? He's as good a papa as papa was."

Clara didn't know whether to laugh or cry at her son's question. Soon to be five, too intelligent for his own good, he knew Jonah would make a wonderful father to both him and Edna . "I'm sorry, sweetheart, but Jonah doesn't belong to our community."

"Why's that matter?" Edna asked. "We love him and he loves us. He said so when we went swimming."

That familiar waterfall of emotions—this time more like one of the waves that flooded the earth in the story of Noah and the Arc—engulfed Clara. *God, please help me,* she prayed silently. *My precious children love a man who would be the perfect father to them—and so do I.* To keep from crying, she clenched her teeth, but hot moisture escaped her eyes.

John touched the corner of one eye. "Don't cry, Mama. God will send a mirkle."

His pronunciation of "miracle" banished Clara's tears. "You're right, God will send a miracle. Now, about that Bible verse. It's—"

"I know," Edna said. "'Proverbs 17:22: A merry heart doeth good like a medicine, but a broken spirit drieth the bones.'"

"Dry bones?" John poked his arm. "I don't want dry bones."

"Good," Edna said. "I can make you laugh all I want to."

Although Clara marveled at her sweet children, they needed a father before they got too old. Whoever that might be in the end, she had no idea. Since Edna had explained Proverb 17:22 so well, Clara stood and took the suitcase to her room, where she opened it on the bed and unpacked everything. The cabin had a washing machine, but she considered her time there a vacation from the work at home. Now she needed to catch up on all the chores.

John and Edna had left while she unpacked the suitcase. The screen door slammed, and his feet pattered into her room. "Mama, Mama! We got baby chicks!"

Edna's feet pattered in also. "And lots of eggs!"

Clara shook her head. She had driven Jonah's pickup here every day to feed and milk the cow, but chicks and lots of eggs were what she got for ignoring the chickens except for feeding them. Maybe that was because her mind had been occupied with thoughts of her predicament with Vernon and Jonah.

She told the children to gather all the eggs while she heated water to wash clothes. Kneeling over the washtub on the back porch, with steam rising up as she scrubbed the clothes on a washboard, she stopped to wipe sweat from her forehead. Since she and Jonah had argued, he might not wire the house for lights and a heat pump, and air conditioning while washing clothes would be wonderful. Then again, a washing machine would remove that workload from her already overworked hands. As far as a dryer, she preferred the smell of fresh air and sunshine in clothes hung on the line to dry. No machine she knew of could provide those aromas; only God could do that.

Done with rinsing the clothes in cold water in the bathtub, she had the children hold each piece while she twisted the water out as best she could. Wiping sweat again, she wished she and Abram had bought a diesel generator to run a washing machine. If they had, like with Alison's washer, it would spin most of the water out, leaving them much lighter and less likely to make the clothesline droop like an old swaybacked mule Papa once had.

The memory brought back his and Mama's concern about Clara living in Virginia instead of near them in Pennsylvania, marrying Noah to do so. The idea held certain attractions, such as having her family close. Another was Noah's handsome, teasing, and smiling self. Although Abram was the love of her life, he faced it with seriousness more than lightheartedness. He did love to laugh, but it took more to pull it from him, similar to a stubborn tooth, its root unwilling to pop loose from a jaw. She loved him because of it. Regardless of the subject, she always knew where he stood.

Jonah, on the other hand, was a mix of both humor and seriousness. Unlike Noah or Abram, however, something either in his brown eyes, his soft smile, or the way his glance could melt her heart—or maybe all three—filled her with hope for the possibility of marrying him. *No,* she thought, as she carried the basket of clothes to the line. That was a dream only, one most young women had when they thought of the perfect husband. There was no such thing for Clara. Vernon would do, and that was that.

Done hanging the clothes on the line, she set her hands on her hips and leaned backward to loosen the knots in her spine. John and Edna, who had been handing her the clothes and clothespins, did the same thing, prompting a huge smile that felt as if it would split her cheeks.

What a blessing they were, drawing her from her

melancholy like Jesus's love draws repentance from a sinner.

On the back porch, Clara dumped the washtub full of dirty water in the grass and turned it upside-down on the weathered boards until the next wash day. John and Edna dutifully carried the clothes basket to the kitchen and set it in a corner. As much as Clara regretted it, she needed to plow the overgrown part of the garden, leaving the few plants that were still bearing, such as tomatoes. Then she needed to plant lettuce, carrots, peas, and radishes for a late harvest.

John and Edna followed her to the tractor. The fuel gauge read half-full. When she climbed aboard, wasps buzzed from beneath the seat. Instead of swatting at the brown cloud, Clara jumped down, ripping her dress on the gear shift lever, and ran after John and Edna, who were screaming about the wasps going to sting them. Miraculously, no one was stung, but the wasps still formed a whirring cloud around the seat.

Clara had no choice; she needed to plow the garden today to have it ready for fall planting. With the children asking what she was going to do, she stomped across the yard, through the gravel, and across the porch into the kitchen, to her phone on the table. "Jonah?" she asked when he answered, "would you please help me with—" Her mouth fell open. The screen said he had ended the call. She twisted her lips one way and then the other. If Mr. Jonah Ellis wanted to act like a child about their disagreement concerning how she had treated Denver at the restaurant, so could she.

Putting John and Edna in the pickup truck, she could feel her cheeks flaring with heat, and it wasn't from the late August sun beaming overhead either.

The rear tires slung gravel. Crowded in the passenger seat instead of their car seats in the rear seat, Edna and John looked at each other wide-eyed. When the tires cleared the gravel driveway, they squawked on the pavement.

Before Clara could shift into third gear, she braked hard and roared into Jonah's driveway, less than 100 steps down the road. The driver's side front bumper hit the mailbox post, sending it and the box into the weeds behind it. Clara stuck her tongue out at it. That's what he got for not keeping his grass cut like a good neighbor should. If he were Beachy Amish instead of English, he would know that.

Continuing down the driveway, Clara stopped. Jonah, trotting toward her from his house, was shading his eyes, no doubt trying to figure out whose vehicle had crashed at the end of his driveway. He stopped at her front bumper and took something from it. She told the children to sit still and slammed the door. "Who are you to hang up on me, Jonah Ellis?"

He waggled the splinter of wood in his hand at her. "Who are you to hit my mailbox? I recognize the white paint on this wood, and I don't see it by the road."

"You shouldn't have hung up on me. What if John or Edna were sick?"

"You shouldn't have asked Denver those stupid questions. What if I wanted to get to know him and his family better and you ruined it?"

"Huh," Clara said, huffing a disgusted breath. "What you want is to get to know that red-headed hussy Tess better."

"What if I do? She wasn't at the restaurant, but at least she didn't insult anyone there like you did. Listen to you, calling a stranger a hussy. That's a doggoned judgmental way for an Amish person to act."

Whirling toward the pickup to leave, Clara whirled back around and closed the distance between her and Jonah. "You just want her because she's got bigger ... well, I won't say, but she does."

"Aw, the poor Amish girl is embarrassed. Sure, Tess has lots of sand in both ends of her hourglass, but I wouldn't date her because of that."

"See? You were looking at her. You men are all the same, lusting after women and thinking immoral thoughts." Clara crossed her arms over her chest, conscious of the lack of sand in upper half of her hourglass. "You make me sick."

Jonah crossed his arms too. "You make me sicker. Admit it, you're just jealous."

As if her lashes were the wings of a butterfly in a hard wind, Clara blinked furiously. "I'd rather marry a goat."

"I'd rather marry a cow. I'm sure she'd be a lot nicer than you."

Clara uncrossed her arms and waggled her finger so close to Jonah's face that the tip touched his nose. "That can be arranged, Jonah Ellis. My cow has enough room in her stall for the both of you."

Jonah grabbed her finger. She waggled the other finger and he grabbed that one too. There they stood, face to face, eye to eye, cheeks red, lips tight.

Until they burst out laughing.

To hold her aching stomach, Clara pulled her fingers from Jonah's grip. Sounding like a braying donkey, he stumbled over to the fence beside his driveway and held onto a post while bending over, laughing even harder. As his laughs dwindled to chuckles, he dropped to his behind and sat with his back against the post.

Clara came over and sat beside him. "I haven't laughed like that since Mama put too much cayenne pepper in a new chili recipe and Papa ate a big spoonful from the pot before supper. He accused her of trying to poison him, and she thanked him for warning us children of her mistake."

Jonah chuckled again. "I wish I had seen that." He faced her. "I'm sorry about our argument at the cabin. Being Beachy Amish, I guess it's hard for you to accept relationships like the one between Denver and Eliza and Tess."

"Are you sorry about criticizing my hourglass? I can't help it if it's low in sand."

"I didn't criticize it. I just said Tess had lots in hers."

"You know what I mean."

Jonah chuckled once more. "I happen to like hourglasses like yours. You'd be easier to carry over the threshold after our wedding."

Edna rolled the pickup window down. "Can we come out? It's getting hot."

"I'll be there in a minute," Clara said. She faced Jonah. "I hope this means we're best friends again. I hate to think of my world without Jonah Ellis in it."

"I feel the same way about you, Clara

Engelman," he whispered.

Above the blades of grass before Clara, a dragonfly hovered back and forth. It's huge, faceted eyes focused on her and Jonah in turn. It's four wings, a blur in the sunlight, reflected rainbow hues if Clara looked hard enough, or either she was imagining it.

"A rainbow before the storm," Jonah said.

She slapped his arm. "You mean *after* the storm, silly."

"Hey," he said, grinning, "when the storm is me and you, there's no difference. Why did you call me?"

Clara looked up into his kind eyes. His closeness tempted her to kiss his cheek. Worse, it tempted her to tears. She could never move back to Pennsylvania and leave Abram here, in his grave beneath the oak behind the house, but living so close to the one man who filled her and the children's ideals of the perfect father and husband was pure torture. "I'm glad we made up," she said, standing. I called because a wasp nest is under the tractor seat. Can you knock it out for me? I want to plow part of the garden to get it ready for fall crops."

Jonah stood too. "Your line is full of clothes. Don't you need to take a break?"

"It wouldn't be such a chore if I had a clothes washer."

"That reminds me," he said, snapping his fingers. "I need to wire your house. I'm sorry I haven't started. I told you I would over a year ago."

"That's all right. You can start whenever you'd like."

The screen door on Jonah's porch slammed. Lydia shaded her eyes from the sunlight slanting down from the horizon. "Did you find out what that noise was?" she yelled

Jonah waved. "Some guy in an old pickup hit the mailbox. Clara saw it happen and stopped to tell me."

"Jonah," Edna hissed, sticking her head out of the pickup window. "You told a lie."

Clara agreed with Edna's assessment. "She's right, you know. Why did you do that?"

Lydia went back inside, and Jonah faced Clara. "She painted that mailbox for my birthday. You might not have noticed, but both sides have dragonflies on them."

"But she didn't get mad."

Consider it a life lesson," Jonah said, winking. "It can be easier to get mad at someone you know than a stranger. I don't like lying, but it wouldn't have done any good to upset her. I've got some wasp spray. I'll be there in a minute."

As Clara drove back home, Edna tapped her arm. "Can I lie now since Jonah lied?"

Clara cut her eyes at her. "You most certainly cannot, young lady."

"But—"

"It's not the same. Jonah's an adult and you're a child. He decided with an adult mind. Children don't always do that."

"Oh. So adults can lie …"

"I don't mean that either," Clara said, frustrated. Both Beachy Amish and the English had their issues. She had known people who lied, and she had heard stories of abuse in the home. Of course, with the help of their faith in God, more Amish fought their human frailties than the English. Alison told her a while back how she had seen a news story in a store in South Boston on a row of TVs for sale. People were burning businesses and attacking each other. People were robbing stores and murdering the owners. People were screaming at each other instead of listening to each other. Such things saddened Clara. No wonder the Amish and Mennonites preferred to stay out of the issues of the English.

"I don't like Jonah anymore," John murmured. "Papa wouldn't lie to us."

Clara said nothing. It was time for another lesson

for her children, one she might do well to understand herself.

At home again, she sat them down on the porch steps and faced them. "You said Jonah told you he loves you when he took you swimming. I love you both and so does he. All people make mistakes. What's important is realizing those mistakes and not repeating them. Jonah lied about the mailbox to protect Lydia's feelings. I won't judge him for that, and I'm sure God won't either."

"What about the commandment?" Edna asked. "Thou shalt not lie?"

John nodded. "That's right, Mama."

Taking a deep breath, Clara closed her eyes. She sometimes felt conflicted about certain biblical doctrine herself, but one thing was clear. She opened her eyes. Two precious faces waited for an answer: blue eyes like Abram's, turned up noses like hers, the slightest splash of freckles on sun-kissed cheeks, expectant expressions mixed with curiosity for her answer, along with their forever look of trust and love. Of all the blessings in her life, being a parent and a mother was one of the best. Now it was time to honor her part in shaping her children's lives so they would become as kind and as caring and as understanding as her and Abram had always tried to be.

A sudden thought burst into her mind, riding

the breeze above the grass beside Jonah's driveway, truth in the promise of the rainbow, hinted in the colors of a dragonfly's wings.

And as kind and as caring and as understanding as her dear friend—her best friend—Jonah was.

Kneeling beside her children, she explained how every person ever born, or to be born, is a sinner. How God sent his Son to take those sins as his own in order to free His children from them, and all they had to do to be free of them was to ask him in Jesus's name. "Furthermore," she added, "God understands the weaknesses born into people, so He understands how hard it is not to sin. He loves us still, even when we sin like Jonah did by lying. "The most important thing," she concluded, "is to recognize our sins as opportunities to become better people by not repeating them. Does that make sense?"

Beaming smiles, her children nodded. "Good," John said. "Now I can like Jonah again."

Edna nudged his shoulder with her. "No, John, we *love* Jonah." She faced Clara. "Right, Mama?"

At the end of the driveway, gravel crunched as Jonah drove toward them.

Clara faced her children again. "You're right, Edna. We *do* love Jonah."

Chapter 9

The following Saturday after breakfast, Clara took her phone from the kitchen table and studied the screen. Vernon had been gone for two weeks and hadn't called. For a man who showed up unannounced at her parent's home in Pennsylvania to ask if he could court her, he had some explaining to do.

At the table, dawdling over toast and milk, John and Edna chattered about the fall garden they would plant today. Wanting to take a moment for herself, Clara went to her room and dropped to the bed to open the nightstand drawer. In the bottom, in an old matchbox, the quartz stone Jonah had given her resembled a tiny white heart. She cupped it in her palm and touched it with a fingertip. Over the past year, her thoughts were more of him than of Abram, or perhaps they had blended together: twin reflections within the mirror of her mind. Her dreams had also suffered this transformation, for she was suffering to embrace him within the moonlit shadows of the long and lonely nights, never really, genuinely, feeling the comforting touch of his embrace, even if only as her best friend.

On the nightstand, beside the oil lamp, her phone's buzzing vibration against the wood startled her. She dropped the tiny white heart, returned it and the matchbox to the drawer, and closed it as if it were the door of a tomb, never to be opened. The phone's screen surprised her with Vernon's number. She raised it to her ear, puzzled why he would call now. "Hello?"

"Ah, Clara, it's good to hear your voice. How are you and the children?" She told him they were fine, adding how she hoped he was fine too, waiting to see if he would explain why he hadn't called before now. "Yes, yes, I'm fine," he continued. "The meeting with the other bishops has gone well." Saying nothing, Clara waited again. "Are you there?" he asked. "You usually aren't so quiet."

"I'm here. The children and I were about to plant our fall garden."

"How's Jonah and Lydia? Well, I hope."

"They're fine." Clara considered telling him about the camping trip to the park and meeting Eliza, Denver, and Tess but decided against it. If he wanted to hide things, she could too.

"What have you been doing the last week?" Vernon asked.

Having had enough of his nonsense, Clara

huffed a hard breath into the phone. "Can you not count?" she blurted, allowing anger to creep into her voice. "You've been gone two weeks, Vernon. Two weeks without a single call to see how I am, not to mention the children. I'm not so sure you want to court me at all. Someone who truly cares for me would call at least every other day."

What could only be the clatter of plastic against a floor suggested he had dropped the phone, shocked at both her temper and her statement. He coughed, cleared his throat and coughed again. "I'm uh … well, I don't have any excuse. All I can do is apologize and call more often this coming week."

Clara paused. Since he was staying another week, let him explain it rather than her asking about it.

"Are you there?" he asked, his voice as plaintive as if he were a little boy waking from a bad dream to ask his mother if she were there.

"I'm here," she said flatly.

Silence. Nothing. Then faint sobbing that melted Clara's icy heart. "Vernon, what is it? What's wrong?" Yes, he cared for her, maybe even more than she had realized.

John came to the bedroom door. "Mama, when can we—" She hushed him, said to go back to the kitchen and wait, and closed the bedroom door.

Vernon's sobs grew fainter and less insistent. Cloth rustled, possible him taking a handkerchief from his pocket. He blew his nose, the sound muffled, followed by a deep sigh. "I apologize for not calling before now. I've … I've been under a lot of stress. I know it's wrong to say, but I think God has forsaken me. If I weren't so dedicated to our community, I would consider leaving the Beachy Amish altogether."

Clara's lips slowly parted. She never would've believed Vernon would consider such a thing. Choosing to wait instead of asking what could be so wrong, she remained quiet.

"I know it's a shock to hear that," he said. "I would never do it, of course, but … well … even a bishop can have his doubts."

Considering her thoughts about Jonah, Clara understood Vernon's statement. "Would you like to tell me about it? That's what people do when they care about each other, you know."

"Mostly it's my wife."

The phone slipped from Clara's fingers. Thankfully, it fell to the bed instead of the floor. Had he really said he was upset because of his wife? Hadn't he said she died? She pressed the phone to her ear again, swallowing to steady her spasming throat. Surely he wouldn't lie to her about his wife being dead, not when he wanted to court her. "Is … I mean … what about her, Vernon?"

"I visited her grave on the way here. It was very upsetting. Although the Beachy Amish marry to uphold custom and to strengthen the community, I loved her more than I can say. I'll be honest, Clara, if I had the chance to be with her again, I would in a heartbeat."

His revelation stunned Clara. He had always been so stoic, so unemotional except for when he showed up at her parent's house, and here he was, admitting to being deeply in love with his wife. This was a good thing, a wonderful thing. Perhaps she could marry for love after all. Only time and a long courtship would tell.

"As you know," she said, hoping he would feel a kinship with her if she admitted something similar, "I understand how that feels. I would give anything if Abram hadn't died."

"Well," he murmured, his voice still somber, "it's good to know we have those feelings in common."

Satisfied as to why Vernon hadn't called before now, Clara felt better. "How much longer will you be away? We have church tomorrow."

"It'll be another week. Samuel is interested in being a deacon. I called him to tell him he could say a few words if he likes. Some bishops might not like it since he isn't a deacon, but I'd rather he fill in for me than anyone else."

Anyone else like a woman, Clara thought. With the death of their eldest man last year, their community was growing smaller instead of larger, leaving two couples including Alison and Samuel. If she and Vernon eventually married, that would make it three couples and the wife of the man who had died, hardly enough to grow a community. They had hoped other Beachy Amish Mennonites would move here. So far it hadn't happened. Although she understood how an Amish woman maintained a specific place in a community, a few things bothered her. One was when Vernon decided a month ago that no woman should bring up the gospel of Jesus to outsiders. Upon his ruling, made in a church service, the four women in their community had given each other quick glances of disapproval. Leading people to God was important, not who did it, and some other Beachy Amish bishops had allowed it. Still, the bishop had the final say, so the women had to accept Vernon's decision.

"What if Samuel isn't there?" Clara asked. "Do we just not have church? That doesn't seem right."

Vernon snorted derisively. "I know you're not

suggesting a woman preach, Clara."

"I didn't say that. I just asked a simple question. Can't we discuss scripture in church without a man watching over us?" Clara had almost asked, *Can't we discuss scripture in church without a man hovering over us a like a hawk?* Thankfully, she hadn't let her rising temper get the best of her.

"I assume you do that now when you're visiting," Vernon huffed.

Clara didn't know. The ladies in her community rarely visited because of their work loads. "The children and I were about to plant the fall garden," she said, ready to end the conversation. "Call when you get home." Without waiting for his goodbye, Clara swiped the phone's screen to end the call. It was wrong to think it, but the more she thought about marrying him, let alone courting him, the more she thought how she might be better off to leave the Beachy Amish and marry a man who treated her as an equal in all things, not just with the work load.

* * *

Sunday morning, Clara parked the old pickup outside of Alison's home for the church service. The last sunrise of August warmed her as she got John and Edna out to straighten her dress and finger his unruly curls into place behind his ears. When they turned toward the front porch, Alison came out and waved. "Fair warning, Clara. Samuel has a bad cold. I'm making him stay in bed until after the service."

Clara climbed the porch steps. "Vernon called yesterday and said Samuel would say a few words." She peeked through the screen door. "All the ladies are here I see. Do you still want to hold the service?"

Alison raised the foil lid on the bowl Clara held. "And miss your macaroni salad for lunch? No way."

Following Alison inside to the kitchen table, Clara rolled her eyes at her friend's reply of *No way*. Yes, English ways were slowly creeping into Amish communities, but most preferred they take their time doing it.

Clara got John and Edna situated in two rocking chairs, telling them to be still when they started rocking. On the bench on one side of the table, Alison's three boys waited patiently, dark hair combed, shirt and pants ironed. If there was one thing Clara valued about being a Beachy Amish parent, it was how they disciplined children with spanking when necessary. On some of her visits to stores in South Boston, she saw and heard children screaming and crying for anything from candy to toys while the parents did nothing. No wonder so many English children were rude, such as with not holding doors for Clara when she and the children went to town. They were perfect examples of "spare the rod, spoil the child."

More women arrived, each carrying a bowl or a covered platter. Clara caught a whiff of fried chicken, which made her mouth water. She also smelled fresh-baked bread and a shoo-fly pie, made with brown sugar and molasses.

One lady had no children yet, being newly married. The other, the elderly woman whose husband had died last year, was alone as well, as her children lived in Indiana. She was sitting in a rocking chair by the fireplace. "Oh, my. These old bones of mine are aching this morning." She looked around. "Where are all the menfolk?"

"Samuel is in the bedroom with a cold," Alison said, coming over.

Laureen, the lady with no children, left the table to come over too. "Gabriel has a cold too. It must be going around."

Mrs. Yoder, the elderly woman, surveyed the room, tilting her head side to side. "I suppose the bishop is still away."

"He called to ask Samuel to say a few words," Alison said. "Since no men are here—"

A pickup rumbled outside. Clara perked her ears up at what might be the sound of Jonah's truck.

Two doors slammed. Alison opened the door, and Lydia and Jonah came in. To Clara's surprise, Lydia wore a dark blue dress nearly to her ankles, with plain leather flats. Jonah was even more surprising. He wore slip-on loafers, dark pants, a plain white shirt, and a wide brimmed straw hat, which he removed. "Good morning. I hope you don't mind if Lydia and I join you." He hung the hat on a peg by the door. "You can't be too careful with this August sun. It'll even burn you in the morning if you stay in it long enough."

"Of course you can join us," Alison said. "Have a seat on the bench at the table."

Doing so, Jonah looked around. "Where's all the men?"

Lydia nudged Jonah's shoulder with hers. "Aren't you lucky? You've got all these women to yourself."

Mrs. Yoder twisted her lips side to side disapprovingly, and Laureen's eyebrows rose to an arch.

"You forget Alison's boys and John," Clara told Lydia. "They count too."

"I know, Clara," Lydia said, her voice teasing. "I'm just joking." She looked behind her at the table. "This is quite the spread of food you have here. Will there be preaching, or do you just get together to eat?"

Alison burst out laughing. "You are so funny, Lydia. I sometimes wonder the same thing myself."

"I like to laugh is all. We should get together sometimes. I can always use a friend who has a sense of humor."

"I love your haircut. My head and ears gets so hot under all this hair of mine. I sometimes wish I could throw my kapp away and cut my hair like yours."

"Blasphemy," Mrs. Yoder grumbled.

"Alison's just talking," Jonah said. "I'm sure she wouldn't cut her hair." He gave Mrs. Yoder a little wave. "We've never met. I'm Jonah and this is Lydia. And you are?"

"Mrs. Yoder, young man, and don't you forget it. You English used to watch me in my papa's store back home. You weren't making fun of my clothes either. I know how you are, with your evil ways."

Jonah's mouth fought between a grin and not grinning. "I can see that, Mrs. Yoder. Your eyes are gorgeous."

She raised a finger, swollen and arthritic, to point. "They weren't looking at my eyes, you rogue. One of them even tempted me. Come to think of it, he looked a lot like you, all broad shoulders and tall as an oak."

Clara had never heard Mrs. Yoder talk so

much—or so openly. Regardless of her tone, her gray eyes glittered with humor. Maybe she was enjoying her interaction with Jonah because she missed her husband. Lydia certainly was enjoying him, smiling at him much more affectionately than a sister should, her eyes as bright as Mrs. Yoder's.

Jonah faced Alison. "No one said where all the men are. Is anyone going to preach?" Alison told him about Samuel and Gabriel having colds, to which he looked around at all the women. "Well, the circus doesn't stop because all the monkeys don't show up. What if we talked instead of someone preaching? I enjoy getting to know people by their favorite scriptures."

"A fine idea," Mrs. Yoder said, settling back in her chair. "You start."

"I was hoping you would start, Mrs. Yoder. After all, you're the most experienced person here."

Her lips pursed into a grin. "Well, since you didn't say I'm the *oldest* person here, I'll go ahead. My favorite is Proverbs 31:25. 'Strength and honor are her clothing; and she shall rejoice in time to come.'"

"Ah," Jonah said, nodding. "That's one of the verses the Beachy Amish use to justify wearing plain clothing."

"It is, but we also have to be strong and

honorable to be on guard for charming men like you, Jonah." Mrs. Yoder chuckled. "Listen to me, calling you by your first name. My papa would switch my legs for that, God rest his soul."

"I'll go next," Laureen said. "Mine is Proverbs 16:29. 'A man of violence entices his neighbor and leads him in a way that is not good.'"

"That's my favorite too," Lydia said, rubbing her crooked elbow.

Clara hadn't thought about Lydia's elbow in a while, nor its scar on the inside, preferring to ignore both it and how neither Lydia nor Jonah had explained it. With the way she was rubbing it while agreeing about the verse, could her arm have been hurt by violence of some sort?

"I don't agree with violence either," Jonah said. "Unlike the Amish and their non-violent attitude, I couldn't stand by while someone hurt me or someone I loved." His cheeks reddened. "If that happened, they would deserve whatever they got." He faced Alison. "How about you, our wonderful host? What's your favorite scripture?"

"Me?" Alison squeaked.

"Yes, you. Being Beachy Amish Mennonite, with boys as well behaved as yours, I'm sure you have a one."

Alison tapped a fingertip to her chin. "Well, I like Proverbs 15:5. 'A fool spurns a parent's discipline, but whoever heeds correction shows prudence.' It might not fit me because I like to tease and laugh, but I know how important discipline is." She smiled at her sons. "And my boys know it too. They're as sweet as can be." She faced Clara. "I'm sure my best friend has one we'd all like to hear, don't you, Clara?"

"I'm interested in Jonah's since he's English. Who knows what he might come up with."

Everyone's gaze left Clara and focused on Jonah. He smiled and laughed. "Well, aren't I the center of attention all of a sudden." He had brought a Bible with him, which rested in his lap. He opened it. "Mine's kind of long, so I need to read it." Pages flipped, softly clattering like red and gold leaves fluttering in an autumn breeze. He stopped. "I read both the King James and the New International versions. This is the International version. It's simpler to me, kind of like how love is meant to be simple. He opened the Bible wider. "Corinthians 13, verses four through seven."

Like those red and gold autumn leaves Clara had thought about, her heart fluttered in her chest. Somehow, although she didn't know how, she knew Jonah would choose Corinthians 13. After all, it was her favorite scripture too.

Jonah cleared his throat. "'Love is patient, love is

kind. It does not envy, it does not boast, it is not proud. It does not dishonor others, it is not self-seeking, it is not easily angered, it keeps no record of wrongs. Love does not delight in evil but rejoices with the truth. It always protects, always trusts, always hopes, always perseveres.'"

Except for the soft breaths of the ladies, silence filled the room. Gazing into Jonah's eyes, Clara had mouthed each and every word, and everyone was now watching her.

"Ah, okay," Lydia said, eyeing Clara. "I think we know what your favorite scripture is too."

Mrs. Yoder fanned herself with her hand. "Is it hot in here, or is it just me?"

Alison opened a window. "It's not just you."

Swallowing the emotion filling her throat, Clara stood. "I don't know about anyone else, but I'm ready for lunch."

John and Edna hopped from the rocking chairs and hurried to the table. Jonah asked everyone to bow their heads while he said the blessing, much simpler and straightforward, thanking God for those who prepared this food and to please use it to nourish their bodies. After a resounding "Amen," plates and glasses were filled, forks and spoons clattered, and satisfied lips were wiped with napkins.

Done with his meal, Jonah took a slice of shoo-fly pie to a window and looked out at the sunny day. Clara returned to her chair to watch him, wondering what he was thinking. In a far corner, Alison and Lydia were talking as if they were long lost sisters, sometimes smiling, sometimes serious, sometimes looking around as if they didn't want anyone to hear them. Once, Alison placed her hand on Lydia's arm and nodded over and over, as if she were making some kind of vow.

Jonah left the window and joined Clara, sitting in a nearby chair. "I enjoyed the pie. Does Vernon like that kind?"

With the rush of emotions Clara had experienced at Jonah's reading of Corinthian's 13, the last thing she wanted to talk about was Vernon. Still, with the emotions he had shown concerning his dead wife, he might stir such feelings in Clara if she gave him the chance during their coming courtship.

She faced Jonah. "If he does, I don't know about it. I never paid any attention to what kind of pie he liked before."

"Are you sure you want to court him?" he asked, lowering his voice. "You didn't seem like it that night in Pennsylvania, when we took that drive."

Looking into Jonah's eyes, the only thing Clara was sure of was how it would break her heart to marry Vernon when she loved Jonah. Tears threatened. She coughed and wiped her eyes, saying she had a tickle in her throat.

Jonah stood. "I shouldn't have asked that. It's not like it's any of my business what you do with your personal life. If you still want me to, I'll wire your house when I can. If Vernon wants to live there after you're married, he'll like it wired, I'm sure."

He left for the window again. Lydia and Alison, still in a corner, both looked his way and then Clara's way. Mrs. Yoder came over to sit in the chair Jonah had left. "What a nice fellow your Jonah is. I'd hate to be Beachy Amish and be in love with an English man." She patted Clara's shoulder. "A thing like that can only break someone's heart, you know."

And that heart is mine, Clara thought.

Still at the table, Laureen filled a plate and called Alison over. "Don't you think Samuel would like something?"

Alison hurried over, the ties of her kapp streaming behind her. "Oh, no, I forgot all about him. That's what I get for talking to Lydia so much."

Joining Jonah, Lydia faced Clara. "I'm so glad Jonah and I came today. Now I have someone to tell all my secrets to."

Considering how Clara knew next to nothing about Lydia, or her relationship with Jonah, or how she hurt her arm, she hoped Alison would share some of those secrets as soon as possible.

In the rocking chairs again, John and Edna were yawning. On the sofa now, Alison's boys were doing the same thing. Although the Beachy Amish didn't care to work on Sundays, they still had to rise early for necessary chores like gathering eggs and milking cows. Clara covered a yawn too. Maybe she was also tired from the emotional day, between listening to Jonah share their favorite scripture and to Mrs. Yoder's admonition of what would happen if an Amish woman fell in love with an English man, not to mention Alison and Lydia's budding friendship.

She stayed long enough to help wash and dry dishes before saying goodbye and loading the children into the pickup.

During the drive home, like a black shroud of mourning, low clouds gathered on the horizon. Raindrops soon dotted the windshield, and Clara turned on the wipers. The *slap-slap, slap-slap* sound mimicked the beat of her heart, hesitant and breaking.

Not only would her daughter go to school soon, growing up entirely too fast it seemed, Vernon would enter Clara's life by courting her. How that would work out, she didn't know, but she needed to try as hard as she could to be a good and faithful Beachy Amish Mennonite woman, trusting in God in all things, especially in who He picked as her next husband.

Chapter 10

Edna came into the kitchen, where Clara was folding Wednesday's washing on the table. "Mama, my dress is too short. My knees are almost showing."

"That's right," Clara said, eyeing the hem of Edna's blue dress. "I need to let the hem out on your dresses so you'll be ready for school Monday."

"I'm glad it's at Alison's house."

Clara knew what Edna meant. She often played with Caleb, Alison and Samuel's youngest boy, on the porch with her dolls, pretending they were a family. "Well, this is school. You can't play with Caleb like you do when you visit or sleep over. You have to learn your math and how to read and write."

Sitting across from Clara, John stopped rolling a toy truck back and forth. "When can I go to school?"

"When you're six like me," Edna said.

"It won't be long," Clara said, folding one of his

shirts. "The next year will fly right by."

Saying nothing, John folded his arms on the table and lowered his chin to his hands. Edna left for the hall, likely going to her room. They had been quiet lately, after Clara told them she would start courting Vernon when he returned from his trip. They hadn't said anything, but she had seen their downturned eyes and mouths, both marking their disappointment. A minute later, John took the toy truck with him, likely for his room as well.

As Clara folded the last piece of clothing—a threadbare dress of hers that she should replace— her phone vibrated in her pocket. She took it out. Vernon was calling, so he might've returned home from his trip early. "Hello, Vernon. Are you done with your business yet?"

"Not quite," he answered. "I just left your parent's house and stopped to get a bite of lunch. I'll start back after that."

"You didn't say you would visit them," Clara said, wondering if he had planned it before he left home.

"I didn't want to bother you with my plans. Your mother introduced me to your old friend, Noah. He seems like a nice fellow. Except for when I went to your parent's house the last time, you never mentioned him, and I was wondering why."

Not knowing how much Mama had told Vernon

about Noah, Clara hesitated.

"Are you there, Clara?"

"I … yes, I am. What did Mama tell you about Noah?"

"Nothing, really. She called him and he came over. He told me about his house behind your parent's house and how you were good friends when you were teenagers."

Clara exhaled a sigh of relief. If this was all Vernon knew about Noah, neither Noah nor Mama had mentioned their feelings for each other when they were younger. Regardless, she wanted to change the subject. "You say you're on your way home. Did you enjoy your trip?"

"It was all right."

Clara didn't understand his answer. He had been so assured about it when he left. Now he sounded as if it didn't matter.

"I missed you," he said. "Do you think we can start our courtship when I get back?"

Noting how he hadn't said he missed the children made Clara hesitate again. That would've been one of the first things Jonah would say, and Noah too. Still, like she had decided, it was time to be the good Beachy Amish Mennonite woman and do her duty for both her children and the community. "Yes, we can start courting."

"Clara, you have made me so happy," he said, his voice excited. "Remember when we talked about visiting the Outer Banks of North Carolina? I just got off the phone with Alison. Since she has kept the children before, and since Edna will go to school Monday, she agreed to keep the children while we go to the Outer Banks."

"Not just us?" Clara asked, trying to keep the panic from her voice. "It's unseemly for us to go alone. Let's wait until school is out. It will look better if the children are with us. We'll tell everyone we'll stay in separate rooms too."

"You're always the Godly woman, one of the things I appreciate about you." Vernon paused, like a man with a surprise. "What if I hire a driver? Then our trip won't raise any eyebrows. Will you, please? We'll get to know each other more in one week than we would in six months otherwise."

Clara couldn't deny that. If Vernon had any faults that wouldn't make him a good husband, she would learn them much faster on a trip than at home. "I suppose we could." Clara paused, wondering who would drive them since their community was so small and all the men were busy. "Who would you like to drive us."

"What if it's a surprise?" Vernon asked, his voice childlike.

Clara smiled, feeling childlike herself. Of course,

Vernon had already asked Jonah to drive them. "Oh," she said, feeling the sudden burst of excitement fading away.

"What is it?" he asked.

Clara hadn't meant to say *oh* out loud. If Jonah drove them, his presence might stop her from giving Vernon the chance he deserved to prove himself a good husband, one who could fall in love with her and her with him. "Won't it be expensive to hire a driver?" she asked, skirting her concern with a hint of dishonesty like Jonah had been dishonest by telling Lydia someone besides Clara had hit their mailbox.

Vernon chuckled. "Don't you think you're worth it? Consider it an early wedding present."

The lack of a question in his request troubled Clara. Any other man she knew would ask for such a trip to be an early wedding present instead of demanding it. Like she had already decided, though, it was time to be a dutiful woman for her community. "All right then, when would you like to leave?"

"Saturday. You can take the children to Alison Friday. We can leave the first thing Saturday morning."

Again, no question, just a demand. Worse than that, she would miss taking Edna to school on

Monday, her first day. Although it would be like any other time she took the children to play with Alison's children, missing Edna's first day of school gave Clara pause. This wasn't something a mother should do, especially not a Beachy Amish mother. Pressure built in her throat. She wanted to defy Vernon, to tell him how she felt about everything. Despite how the English thought Amish wives were meek and obeyed their husband's orders without question, most couples she knew discussed things. If she and Vernon were married, she would voice her concerns, but him being her bishop created an unease in her heart, as if she were supposed to obey him more as a single woman than as if they were married. How strange a thing, to feel under the thumb of someone not yet a part of her household. Still, she finished the call by saying she would follow his plan, resulting in his affirmation of them having a wonderful time on their trip, even with a driver chaperoning them everywhere.

To let Jonah know about the trip, she called him. He spoke flatly, saying he wished her and Vernon well at the beach, his voice carrying the soft melancholy of a mourning dove cooing in search of a mate from the oak in the back yard on a summer afternoon. He didn't mention driving her and Vernon to the Outer Banks, so maybe Vernon had told him not to say anything to keep it a surprise.

Then he perked up, even snapping his fingers. "What if I start wiring your kitchen while you're gone? If I do, I'm sure I can finish it in a week, even with taking care of the cattle and doing other wiring work."

Clara's spirit lightened at his boyish tone; then it fell like a crow shot from the sky. Whoever Vernon had hired to drive them wasn't Jonah. She told him she would leave a key under the back porch mat so he could get in to work and started to end the call, but he asked her to hold on. "I sort of forgot about it in the excitement of knowing I could start wiring your kitchen. I'm going to start guitar lessons with Tess Saturday morning. She's even letting me borrow one of her beginner guitars free. Isn't that nice of her?"

The attractive Tess, with her full figure, red hair, and green eyes, made Clara wince. In all her life she had never felt jealousy, which now made her clamp her eyes shut and shake her head. "Well," she said, opening her eyes, "I hope you enjoy the guitar."

"I'm sure I will. Tess has invited me to supper that night too. She says she can cook a mean meal on a grill. Her house overlooks the lake, and I'm looking forward to it. Eliza and Denver are keeping her kids so we can have quiet for our first lesson."

Feeling helpless to control both her path in life

and Jonah's, Clara didn't know what to say. The clock over the stove *tick-tocked* several seconds before she could think of a reply. "That's nice of Denver and Eliza. I'm sure Tess wants her children back early. They'll need their sleep before church in the morning."

"They're taking them to church. Tess said she has some guitar work to catch up on. She wants to show me her collection too. I'm looking forward to it."

Clara clenched her hands until the pain of her nails biting into her palms made her stop. That was the second time Jonah had said he was looking forward to being with Tess, except this time their day together might last until the next morning.

She ended the call, saying she would keep in touch from the Outer Banks, then immediately regretted something she had missed: Jonah had made no mention of Lydia going with him to see Tess.

What, exactly, was their relationship? And what, exactly, had happened to her arm? One thing about it: she must not mind him spending time with Tess alone. Clara dredged up a sigh from the pit of her stomach. If he and Lydia were in a relationship, and if she didn't mind him spending time with Tess, she didn't have a jealous bone in her body, while Clara's body was filled with them. How many faults crept within her soul, taking bites from it with the fangs of a demon named Jealousy? Entirely more than the average Beachy Amish Woman, no doubt.

Another sigh hissed from Clara's lips. Along with missing Edna's first day of school, she regretted not being at home with Jonah while he worked in the kitchen. They could talk and smile, laugh and discuss Bible verses. If they did those things, it might remind him of how he shouldn't sin with Tess during their guitar lesson. Clara could even make him lunch, and she could pretend they were married. *No,* she thought, hanging her head in shame. *Thinking such things is wrong in every way possible.* She would have to spend extra time on her knees tonight, asking God to strengthen her against her weak woman's ways, as well as the terrible jealousy taking bites from her soul.

* * *

Saturday morning, no sooner than Clara had packed her suitcase, Vernon called from outside the closed front door. "Clara? We're here." She lifted the heavy suitcase from her bed. Although she looked forward to seeing the ocean, if she hurt her back, she could stay and see if Jonah came home after his guitar lesson with Tess tonight.

Vernon banged on the door. "Are you there? It's

time to go."

In the kitchen, Clara eyed the clock over the stove. Vernon was ten minutes early. "I'm coming," she said, half dragging, half carrying the suitcase. No pain twinged in her back, unfortunately. She opened the door.

Removing his hat, Vernon smiled. "Look at you, lovely as the morning." He stepped aside. "I think you know our driver."

Clara stumbled backward. "Noah?"

"At your service," he said, coming in to get the suitcase.

"But … but …"

He winked. "Vernon will tell you. It'll make sense then. Let me get this in the trunk."

In the kitchen, Vernon faced Clara. "Why are you so surprised? Well, shocked is a better word. Your mother said you and Noah were good friends growing up. He wanted to see the ocean, so I hired him."

It all made sense now to Clara. Mama wanted Noah to interfere with Vernon's courtship, preferably to return to Pennsylvania with Clara as his wife. She locked the front door and hurried to a strange car. As the men climbed in front, leaving her with no other choice than to sit in back alone, she clenched her teeth. As far as she was concerned, she wouldn't have either one of them if they begged on their hands and knees.

Noah clicked his seatbelt and turned around. "How do you like my new car? I bought it especially for this trip."

"It's a little sporty for my taste," Vernon said. "We Beachy Amish aren't supposed to draw attention to ourselves."

Clapping Vernon on the shoulder, Noah laughed. "Come on now, I can see you driving my Mustang. The red would match your cheeks." He faced Clara again. "I bought it used in case you were wondering. You know how we try to live within our means."

Clara held in a giggle at how Noah's teasing had made Vernon's cheeks red. Maybe this trip, despite her mother's busybody ways, would be interesting after all. She started to click her seatbelt but stopped. "Wait a minute," she told Noah. "I forgot something." She got out and ran to the oak tree in the backyard, where Abram's white cross brought tears to her eyes. Yes, she had been away on the trip to Pennsylvania, but this trip, since it was the beginning of her courting Vernon, felt like it might take place on the moon. She dropped to her knees, not caring if the grass stained her dress or not, and folded her arms around the cross. "Please don't be upset if I marry again," she said, trying to hold back a sob. "I'll always love you no matter what, because you taught me the meaning of love."

Overhead, the oak leaves rustled although no breeze blew. She looked up into the sunlight filtering down through the branches. If she didn't know any better—and she didn't—Abram was blowing her a breathless kiss. Whether it meant he understood about her marrying again wasn't clear, but she took it as a blessing.

She stood and wiped her eyes with the hem of her dress. Over the hill between her house and Jonah's, standing on his porch, he waved. Was this Abram's suggestion hidden in his breathless kiss? Did he want her to marry Jonah because he knew he was the one man living who would make her as happy as he had during the short time they were married?

She waved also. He waved once more and raised a hand to his face. Was he wiping his eyes? It was too far to tell. If he loved her like she loved him, why not tell her? It was her turn to wipe her eyes again. What a stupid thing to think when she was Beachy Amish and he was English, each as far apart from each other as if they lived on the opposite sides of the earth instead of living just over a hill from each other.

She returned to Noah's car. At the end of her driveway, he turned right. When his car passed

Jonah's driveway, his pickup was coming toward the main road. Clara turned to look behind her. Jonah was following them, but not too close. Part of her, the unreasonable part, wished he would force the red Mustang off the road and tell her she was making a mistake, but that in itself would be a mistake. They lived in two different worlds. Even if he admitted to loving her, their situation was impossible. Clara turned back around. How many times did she have to tell herself that before it sank into her hard head?

They soon turned onto highway 15. Miles later, at the end of the business bridge that crossed the lake to Clarksville, Noah turned left on highway 58, and Jonah continued across the bridge. It was too early for his guitar lesson with Tess; maybe he needed something in town.

The entire time, Vernon and Noah had been quiet. Knowing Noah like she did, and her mama, Clara wondered what kind of plan they had hatched to ruin the trip to the Outer Banks, including the courtship that was just beginning.

They passed the entrance to Occoneechee State Park. Ten minutes later they passed Boydton. In South Hill, Vernon bought coffee and breakfast biscuits for everyone at a fast-food place. Beneath the car's whirring tires, the miles fell away. With a full stomach, Clara grew drowsy as the morning sun rose high enough to warm the inside of the car.

Noah finished his coffee and handed the cup back, possibly expecting her to put it in the bag to throw away without asking. Clara took the cup. "It's nice to be thought of as the trash woman."

Vernon handed his cup back. "Thank you, Clara."

Shoving the cups in the bag, she twisted her lips one way and then the other. The English had a saying about this, so Alison had told her. *Men: you can't live with them; you can't live without them.*

Noah glanced at Vernon. "You mentioned seeing some wild horses. Where are they exactly?"

"Corolla," Vernon said. "It's spelled like the car but not said the same. Caw-raw-la."

Noah sputtered laughter. "Do crows live there?"

"I suppose, why?"

To keep from sputtering herself, Clara pursed her lips. Poor Vernon wouldn't know a joke if a crow swooped out of the sky and told him one. Noah, on the other hand, knew too many of them. On their walks as teenagers, by the time she got home, her stomach would ache from laughing.

"No reason," Noah said, looking at Clara's reflection in the rear-view mirror. She couldn't see his mouth, but she knew he was grinning.

"What's so funny?" Vernon asked, tension in his

voice.

"Oh, nothing," Noah said. "Nothing at all."

More miles passed. Not long after a sign noting the city limits of Suffolk, Noah turned right, following his GPS's female voice. "That's quite a contraption," Vernon said. "If I had used one instead of a map, maybe my trip to Clara's parent's home wouldn't have been so nerve wracking near Washington D.C. It made me want to pull my hair out."

Noah glanced his way. "You don't want to do that. Your hairline is receding now. How old are you, if you don't mind me asking?"

"I don't mind. Age is akin to wisdom."

"Oh, really? Then how wise are you? I'm twenty-eight years wise myself, and Clara is twenty-six."

"I'm thirty-eight, proud of every year."

Clara cut her eyes back and forth between the men. Noah, obviously, was trying to make her see how Vernon was too old for her. Thirty-eight *was* a bit advanced. If they were married by the time he was forty, any children they might have wouldn't be old enough to marry until he was almost sixty.

"Don't you mean you're blessed by every year instead of saying you're proud?" Noah asked. "We Beachy Amish aren't supposed to be prideful."

"Well," Vernon said, rubbing his chin, "that's

what I meant. I just used the wrong word."

Silence followed their exchange. Nearing a convenience store on the left, Noah pressed the turn signal lever. "When I researched this route for the GPS on the internet, I learned this place has fried chicken gizzards."

That's a good idea, Clara thought. *Then you can chew on something else besides Vernon.*

Inside the store, which smelled of hot oil, they all took turns in the one bathroom. Noah bought an order of gizzards and a soft drink. Vernon started to buy an order of fried chicken livers but said he wouldn't because they gave him gas. Instead, he bought a bacon, lettuce, and tomato sandwich. As he paid, Noah asked Clara if she was hungry. Vernon apologized for not asking her, adding how he was in a hurry to get out of the hot oil smell. She told him she loved fried chicken livers but hadn't had any in years. He said even the smell made him burp. Noah bought her an order and a soft drink. Vernon eyed them both but said nothing.

On the road again, she and Noah crunched their fried foods and swallowed soft drink while Vernon ate his sandwich, washing the bites down with a carton of milk he had bought.

They soon left this road, turning left onto highway 158. "All right," Noah said. "This road takes us right to the Outer Banks."

Vernon leaned close to the GPS on the dashboard. "This says we're going to Elizabeth City. Is that on the Outer Banks?"

In the rear-view mirror, Noah's blue eyes glinted with humor. "You know about those wild horses. Why don't you know about Elizabeth City?"

"I researched the horses on my phone. I didn't research Elizabeth City."

"You didn't research the route?"

"I knew I wasn't going to drive."

Noah touched the GPS screen. "That little blue car is us. That line is the route. It stops at Corolla. That means we'll go through Elizabeth City."

"Oh," Vernon said, his tone like that of a child who had been corrected by a teacher.

In Elizabeth City, a much larger town than any Clara had visited, they passed more fast-food places. At the third one, Vernon pointed, telling Noah he needed a restroom. No one else had to go, so they waited in the car. After five minutes, Noah turned in his seat to face Clara. "I suppose his sandwich upset his stomach."

Clara smacked his arm on the back of his seat. "You behave. You've harassed him ever since we left home."

"Uh-huh, and you laughed every time I did. Why are you courting him, Clara? You know he's too old for you. You don't have anything in common. He's not particularly handsome. His hair line is receding and is turning gray at the temples. He's getting fat too."

"Looks aren't everything," she replied.

"No, but it's something." Noah raised his eyebrows several times. "Don't you like my blue eyes better than his muddy brown ones? You used to like them when I walked you home after a singing."

With his arm hanging over the back seat, his blond hair wavy and handsome, his blue eyes twinkling, Clara had to admit that being good-looking, like with Abram, had its attractions in a marriage.

Noah laughed. "I see you thinking about it. We'll have to take a moonlight walk on the beach after old man Vernon goes to bed early one night, or *more* than one night. I might even steal a kiss or three before we head back home."

Clara hesitated. Although she had thought about kissing Noah on their walks, she hadn't thought about it since then. Now, as he teased and laughed, those old feelings rushed in again, made even stronger because of the differences between him and Vernon. Regardless, as she had grown older and wiser, she had learned how feelings could get a person into trouble. Didn't the English have problems with out of wedlock pregnancies and fatherless children? They certainly did. All the Amish and Mennonites weren't perfect, but they, on the whole, valued families more than many of the English did, who wondered why their society was breaking down. Clara had heard several conversations in the grocery store concerning this, from how children refused to behave in schools, to how parents thought it was the teacher's fault, to how fewer and fewer people were deciding to teach, plus the rising number of them who were leaving the once honored profession. One woman had even told another how she had been physically attacked by a student, shocking Clara as she waited at the register behind them. Just the idea of it was upsetting, much less it actually happening.

"Look at you," Noah said. "You've gone into a trance thinking about my kisses."

"Hush," Clara said, pointing outside the car. "Vernon's coming."

Noah turned around. Hurrying through the parking lot, Vernon hitched his pants. "Huh," Noah said. "He looks like he should've stayed in the bathroom a little longer. What a sour look on his old face."

"Stop it," Clara said, trying not giggle. "Don't be so rude."

"Then you stop hee-hawing like a mule. You know how I used to love making you laugh. You'd be happier if you married me and you know it."

Grunting as if his stomach was hurting, Vernon got in the car. Clara leaned forward, placing a hand on his shoulder. "Are you all right?"

"I think so," he said, buckling his seatbelt.

Noah waved his hand in front of his face. "I smell a skunk. Does anyone smell a skunk? I smell a skunk. An *old* skunk at that."

Clara shoved his shoulder. "The only thing I smell is a baby who's dirtied his diaper. Let's go."

As they continued on their journey, Clara looked out the window. If Noah kept making her laugh, her old feelings for him might return even more. How could she marry a man like Vernon, whose sense of humor was almost nonexistent? After all, Proverbs 17:22 said a 'merry heart doeth good like a medicine: but a broken spirit drieth the bones.'

With that poignant scripture ringing in her mind, she wondered what their coming time on the Outer Banks would bring. If anything, Noah's joking would certainly keep the boredom away.

Chapter 11

After leaving Elizabeth City, Noah occasionally studied Clara's reflection in the rear-view mirror. No doubt she had guessed his and her mother's plan. Her part in it was simple: have him break up the courting couple so she would give up on living in Virginia and come home. His part wasn't so simple: have her fall in love with him so they could marry. Regardless of where they lived, she had been his dream from the first time he had walked her home after a singing. Softspoken and beautiful, with flaming hair like the fire of love in his soul that still burned for her, she had entered his heart and had never left. Yes, he had loved the other woman he had courted—it broke his heart when she ended their relationship, saying she could see he was in love with someone else—but he didn't dare admit it. He hated lying to Clara about it, saying the break up was his fault. Still, his honor as a Beachy Amish Mennonite man demanded he not belittle his former love.

The miles rolled on, evidenced by the soft hum

of the tires on the road. Clara's reflection faced the window.

To Noah's left, so a sign had said, part of the Dismal Swamp formed a backdrop of a type of tree Noah had never seen. Toward the bottom, the trunks, gray like a dreary Pennsylvania sky spitting sleet, splayed like fingers on a hand. From reaching limbs reflecting in water as black as coffee, some type of moss the same eerie gray draped liked shrouds. On logs extending from the water, turtles both small and large sunned in rows. Right beside the highway, which humped in the swamp like a mule's back, no trees grew in the black water for about fifty yards. Every now and then, what resembled a fence post extended upward. About halfway up the posts, an inverted metal funnel would keep snakes from slithering up the pole and taking eggs or hatchling from what could only be houses for wild ducks.

"Oh, my," Clara said behind him. "That swamp gives me the shivers. I'm sure it's filled with snakes."

"I can't stand snakes myself," Noah said, glancing at Vernon. "Much less a snake in human form."

Vernon cut his eyes toward Noah. "What do you mean?"

"Well, I mean like Amish and Mennonite men

who mistreat their wives and children. We all hear those stories. I think it's despicable."

"That's the weakness of man," Vernon said. "If those men ask for forgiveness, we must accept it and move on."

Noah hesitated. If his inquiries into Vernon's past turned up any lies concerning his wife's death, *he* would be the one asking Clara's forgiveness. Regardless, Noah was sure she wouldn't marry a liar.

He glanced at Vernon again. "What if they don't ask forgiveness, Vernon? Maybe you've met some men like that. The ones I've heard about are shunned. You might know, but what happens to the wife of a man who's shunned? If he leaves the Amish and divorces her, he can remarry in the English world but she can't in the Amish world. Do you know of any situations like that? It's not very fair to her when she hasn't done anything wrong."

A muscle in Vernon's jaw twitched. "I've never known of an instance when a man like that didn't see the error of his ways and didn't receive forgiveness. I hope I never live to see otherwise."

Noah said nothing. He had heard a rumor by a woman visiting from the community where Vernon was born, who said his wife had divorced him. She didn't say if it were true or not, only that it was a rumor. Ever since Noah had learned of Clara's intention to court Vernon, he had wanted to delve into it further. It might be the final straw that broke their courtship, but he needed evidence before he could use it. Another thing pointed to Vernon's strange past: he had moved around several times over the last ten years, as if he were trying to escape a tragedy. Of course, that tragedy could be his wife divorcing him, which would mean he could never marry again by Amish or Mennonite standards.

Although that scenario might help Noah regain Clara, he sympathized with Vernon. He seemed to be a decent bishop, caring for his community as well as caring for Clara. To be denied love because his wife had turned her back on him would be a nightmare. But what if he had mistreated his wife, which had led to the divorce? If so, Clara should know, and the sooner the better.

About twenty minutes later, Clara tapped the back of his seat. "Let's stop at that farm market with the windmill. I've been seeing signs for their peach yogurt."

"I agree," Vernon said, twisting his head side to side while rubbing his neck. "I'm stiff from all this riding."

Noah chuckled. "Well, you are older than Clara and I."

"And wiser," Clara said, defending him. "No matter how old some people get, they act like children."

Vernon's shoulders rose and fell with must be several silent chuckles. "She got you there, young man. I'll take wisdom over youth any day of the week."

Whatever, old man, Noah thought. *If this young man finds out you're lying to Clara about your wife, he'll find out soon enough.*

Several cars were parked at the market, where green awnings shaded its perimeter. Inside and outside, studying tables filled with various fruits and vegetables, shoppers milled around, visible through huge open doors like garage doors. Vernon led Clara to the yogurt stand in a smaller building to the right. Noah found a restroom in back of the market. When he returned, Vernon and Clara were sitting at a small table outside the yogurt stand, in the shade of a vine of some kind, it's tendrils and foliage twisting overhead. Like the vine, jealousy twisted in Noah's chest. He should be sitting with her, not old man Vernon. Offering a silent prayer to ask forgiveness for his jealousy, he joined the shoppers in the market.

The aroma of fresh baked goods drew him to a back room, past a fudge counter. Behind another counter, a woman was pressing a pie crust into a pan, while another was boxing some kind of pastry. At a table by the counter, in front of a plate of samples, a sign identified them as scones.

Licking his lips, Noah chose a pecan pie. Done paying for it, he found Vernon and Clara still at the table. The yogurt cups were empty, so why were they still sitting there with everything to see in the market? Vernon said something, and Clara laughed. Whatever they were talking about, she was enjoying it entirely too much. Noah hurried over and sat the pie before Clara. "I remembered how pecan pie is your favorite."

"Thank you," she said, "but that was years ago. My favorite is peach now." She touched Vernon's hand on the table. "Vernon was just telling me how he had researched this market on his phone a while back and had forgotten they sell peaches when they're in season."

Vernon smiled. "And I said she would be the sweetest peach here, in season or out."

Jealousy twined around Noah's heart once more. The old man knew how to be charming, but he would never outcharm his driver. There would be plenty of opportunities for that during this trip. After all, old man Vernon would need to go to bed early for his aches and pains, leaving the young people to walk barefoot on the beach in the

September moonlight, possibly even daring to hold hands.

The thought tightened Noah's chest. How could he have let Abram take Clara from him? Regret closed his throat. Heartache tempted him to tears, but he refused to let his sadness show. Still, Clara's happiness was more important than his. If she were to truly love Vernon, or any other man, returning to Pennsylvania was his only option.

When they were on the road again, silence filled the car. Vernon tapped his finger on his thigh. A brief smile passed over his face. In the rear-view mirror, Clara's reflection smiled also. Noah clenched his teeth. Surely she wasn't in love with Vernon already, but such happy feelings must be dealt with. After a seafood supper, which they had discussed during the drive, the old man might be ready for bed. If so, that walk on the beach would determine Clara's feelings for him, at least in this early stage of their courtship.

* * *

Leaving Noah's car after a supper of delicious broiled flounder, Clara continued to her hotel room, one of two Vernon had rented. When Noah learned he didn't have a room to himself, he had frowned, saying he preferred his privacy. Vernon replied by saying Noah needed to learn to be frugal. After unpacking, they had gone out to eat, not even having time to walk to the gazebo behind the motel for a view of the beach from the top of a sand dune.

At her door now, about to open it with a plastic card that slid into a metal slot above the knob, she paused. From the beach, the crash of the waves, the cry of the gulls, and the aroma of salt on the breeze drew her like a bee to a bloom. She didn't care to go alone, feeling strange about being in a different place. Both Vernon and Noah had already entered their room, so she did the same. They were on the bottom floor of a seven-story building. Her room also had a door on the other end. She went to it, curious as to where it went, and clasped her hands to her chest after she opened it.

Two walls enclosed a small area, where two chairs waited for a vacationer or two. About ten steps from the chairs, a retaining wall supported sand at the beginning of the dune where the gazebo stood. On the sloped sides and peak of the dune, tall stems bowed in the breeze. At their tips, rows of a grain similar to oats reminded her of them back home in Pennsylvania.

In this small cubby hole, the crash of the waves seemed to engulf her. Several gulls, wings like slender white knives, passed by. Starting just above the dune, pink sunlight rimmed the horizon, lightening to blue toward the few whisps of cloud in a cobalt sky. What a glorious sunset, but how glorious might it be toward the west, across that amazing body of water called the Albemarle Sound? Although the nearly three-mile-long bridge Noah had driven across on the way here had intrigued her, it didn't compare to the vast body of water, its surface shimmering in the late afternoon sun.

To her right, along the sandy path leading up to the gazebo, a young man and woman climbed the dune, hand in hand. Beneath the gazebo, he placed his arm around her shoulders and pulled her close as they watched the ocean.

Clara blinked at the two people, able to show their affection out in public. She knew it was wrong to question Beachy Amish traditions, but what did it hurt to simply hold a loved one's hand or place an arm around their waist or shoulders? Such actions brought married couples closer, which would create a stronger community overall. Regardless, she and other women had no say so in the matter, deferring to the religious leaders, the bishops and the deacons.

The man and woman faced each other, spoke words that were carried away on the soft breeze, and kissed.

Clara turned away, cheeks burning with embarrassment and—envy?

Yes, she envied this couple. They were so much like her and Abram at home in the days following their wedding, when they were getting to know each other: teasing, playing, touching, loving. Late at night, as she lay in bed thinking about him, she still sometimes missed him to the point of tears. She thought the pain of his passing would've lessened by now—it had for the most part—but not the physical yearning to hold someone close, sharing a lingering hug and kiss.

Retreating from the tender scene of the couple in the gazebo, she returned to the room. As she sat on the bed to remove her tennis shoes, her phone on the nightstand vibrated. The screen showed a text from Jonah.

How do you like the beach?

I haven't seen it yet.

Really? What's wrong with Vernon? That's the first thing I would've showed you.

As caring as Jonah was, Clara didn't doubt his words one bit. *We'll see it tomorrow.*

Who's your driver? He looked closer to your age then Vernon's.

Clara had never told Jonah about Noah, not at home or that night in Pennsylvania when they took that drive. *Vernon surprised me with him. He's an old friend of my parents.*

How did that come about?

Vernon visited them on his trip. My mother suggested the driving arrangement.

Lol. It sounds like your mother wants you to marry this old friend and move back home.

Clara texted nothing.

Are you there?

Yes. Clara's fingertips hovered over the phone. What would he say if she said she missed him?

I started wiring the kitchen this morning after you left. I went to town for one of those lights you wear on your head so I could see better. You don't want to mess around when you're working with wiring.

So that was why he had followed them to the intersection at Clarksville.

Your driver is a handsome guy. Do I need to worry about losing my neighbor?

As much as Clara hated it, she'd rather know about Jonah's evening with Tess. *How did your guitar lesson go?*

We never got around to it. We ate grilled chicken and tossed salad and drank white wine on the dock. The sunset over the lake was amazing. Tess is one of nicest women I've ever met. She has one of those firepits on her deck. She lit that when it got dark, and we talked and talked. She's an amazing woman, talented and a great parent. She played guitar and sang me a beautiful love song she wrote. I could listen to her all night long.

Clara noted Jonah's use of *amazing* concerning his night with Tess. *Well,* she typed, wishing she could add sarcasm to a text, *it sounds like you had an amazing evening.*

We did. She won't even let me pay for the lessons. Since I didn't have one, I'm going back tomorrow night. Denver and Eliza offered to keep Tess's kids again so we can be alone. Jonah paused. *Lol. If we get around to a lesson, that is. Just sitting and talking with her is amaz—*

I know, Clara interrupted, pecking at the phone like a hen after an earthworm, *amazing.* Shaking her head, she chewed her lower lip. As far as she was concerned, she was amazing too, so why hadn't Jonah ever told her so?

Someone knocked on the hotel room door. "Clara? It's Noah."

Are you there, Clara? In case you didn't know it, I miss you.

Regret filled Clara's throat. She should've never promised to court Vernon. If she hadn't, a miracle might've occurred to bring her and Jonah together.

You sure are quiet. Alison called Lydia today. She said John and Edna are fine. She and Lydia have become good friends.

Noah knocked again. "Clara? I got a flashlight

from the car. I thought you might want to take a walk on the beach."

I've got to go, Jonah. Goodnight. Clara shut the phone off and opened the door. "I was just getting ready for bed, Noah."

"Aw, come on," he said, using his teasing tone. "The salt air might help us sleep better."

From behind Noah, a man cleared his throat. "You didn't say you were going to walk on the beach with Clara, Noah. Do you think that's proper?" Vernon looked in the door. "I don't think it's proper, do you, Clara?"

"I was getting ready for bed."

"You and I could take a walk on the beach. After all, *we're* courting. Not you and Noah."

Noah eyed Vernon. "How is you walking on the beach with her any more proper than me walking on the beach with her? I told you, we're old friends."

Standing there with her hand on the doorknob, Clara knew what it must feel like to be a duckling in one of those boxes atop one of those posts in the Dismal Swamp. Two snakes, one named Vernon, the other named Noah, were slithering upward, trying to pass the inverted metal funnel to see which one would gobble her up first. As she waited to see which one would attempt the first bite, by taking her to the beach for a walk, Jonah's face hovered above them: his smile, the cleft in his chin, his earth-brown eyes, his perpetually tanned skin from working with his beef cattle. He had never treated her like a duckling to be gobbled up. He respected her. He valued her. He treated her as an equal.

Throwing her shoulders back and standing tall, she faced the two snakes at her door. "It's our first day here." She touched Vernon's arm. "Noah's an old friend. I see no harm in us strolling the beach to revisit our childhood while we're here. You, on the other hand," she said, touching Noah's arm, "must understand Vernon and me. We're courting, so we need time to get to know one another. That means we need our time alone also." She took a step back from the doorway. "Do you both understand?"

Not waiting for an answer, she closed the door and grinned.

Now they knew how it felt to be the wife of a bossy Amish or Mennonite husband. Let them put *that* in their wide-brimmed hats and wear them.

Giggling, she ran to the bed and buried her face in the pillow before the two snakes could hear her laugh.

Jonah, no doubt, would be proud of her spunk.

Chapter 12

The next night after supper, Clara sat on the bed to undress for a shower. Although she had enjoyed seeing the wild horses that lived on the beach and in the twisted trees and among the houses north of the town called Corolla, the sun and the bouncy ride on the elevated tour vehicle along the beach had worn her out.

Removing her tennis shoes, she stopped when someone knocked on the door. "Clara? It's Noah."

Clara opened the door. "I'm tired and—"

Noah offered her a small container. "Remember how you loved strawberry ice cream when we were young? I walked to a store down the road and bought us some." From his shirt pocket, he offered her a plastic spoon.

Clara noticed the intimate suggestion that they eat out of the same container with the same spoon. She took the container and spoon. "That's very nice of you. You should've bought a container for yourself."

Noah took the top off the container. "I already

ate my half," he said, grinning. "You didn't think I would eat from the same spoon that touched the lips Vernon has kissed, did you?"

Clara ignored the question. Noah knew perfectly well she hadn't kissed anyone since Abram. The English might behave in such a way, like with Jonah, who had probably kissed Tess during their so-called guitar lesson, but the Beachy Amish standards were higher. Creamy and cold, the ice cream was delicious. She finished it while Noah watched, then returned the empty container. "Thank you. I'm sure you won't mind throwing that away."

Noah came inside and dropped it in a trash container. "There you go." He offered her his elbow. "Take my arm for our walk on the beach. You did tell Vernon we could, remember?"

Tempted to shove him out the door, Clara instead looped her arm in his. "I suppose I have to."

She patted her pocket to verify the key card in it, kicked off her tennis shoes and closed the door. Noah led her up the sandy incline to the gazebo, where they stood on the worn and gray wooden boards barefooted. "This is my first time seeing the ocean," he said. "I'm glad it's with you."

The breeze off the water blew the ties of Clara's kapp over her shoulders, bringing the wonderful smell of the Atlantic, almost like the brine mixture she used for soaking pickles. On the horizon, the sky, turning dark above the waves, followed by purple above, then to red, orange, and yellow, foretold of the sunset. As beautiful as the waves were, crashing upon the beach, she turned to face the sunset over the sound in the west, and the view nearly took her breath. "Oh, Noah," she said, "it's beautiful."

He said nothing, simply turned to enjoy the sunset like her. Distant clouds, like God's own paintbrush, tinted the horizon a deep, dark ochre. The sky above it brightened to red, then gradually transformed into dusk.

Although Noah liked teasing her, he had his serious side too, like now, with his silence. Whenever that happened, she knew he was going to ask her something, and she never had to wait long.

"I know I told you why, but I'm sorry I didn't come to Abram's funeral."

His solemn tone surprised Clara. "I wish you had come, Noah. I could've used a friend."

"Vernon tells me you have good friends in your neighbors."

"I didn't know them then."

"How well do you know the man? Jonah, right? Your mother said he drove you and the children when you visited last year?"

"I know him well enough. Mama might've told you about Edna's spider bite. It was a Black Widow. If it hadn't been for Jonah taking us to the emergency room, I hate to think what might've happened."

"Well," Noah said, his voice lowering in tone a notch, "I'm glad he was there for you."

Clara recognized Noah's change in voice. When their feelings were growing for each other as teenagers, he had used that same tone whenever he asked about some boy talking to her. If he had one fault beside his teasing, it was jealousy. Despite their Ordnung's rules against violence, he even threatened to fight a boy once. Then she met her kind and sweet Abram, and all romantic thoughts of Noah had melted like frost on a sunny morning.

The sun lowered beneath the horizon. In the gazebo, a single lightbulb winked on. Noah turned her around by her shoulders to face him. "You're my biggest regret, Clara. I'll never love another woman like I loved you." He paused, swallowing hard. "When you started courting Abram without telling me why, I wondered what I had done. Then I remembered how my jealousy got the best of me when I threatened to fight that boy. Is that why you chose Abram over me?"

"It is," Clara said, admiring how he had

recognized his fault. Unfortunately, she wondered if he had recognized it enough to do something about it, evidenced by his tone a moment ago concerning Jonah.

"I thought so." Noah pointed at the darkening horizon over the ocean. "I see the lights of two ships. I suppose they'll pass each other like we did."

Noah's regret saddened Clara. If he had changed from the jealous boy of the past to the confident man of today, she could see courting him again if it weren't for Vernon. She was tempted to tell him so, but she didn't want to give him false hope. Vernon deserved a chance; fairness and honor demanded it.

She patted Noah's hand on the gazebo's wooden railing. "Thank you for the ice cream and our talk. I'm glad you see how jealousy is a terrible thing." As the words left Clara's lips, shame burned the nape of her neck. If Noah could recognize and stop his fault of jealousy, why couldn't she stop being jealous over Tess's attention to Jonah?

Coming up the path toward the gazebo, Vernon cleared his throat. "Well, now. I think it's my turn to have our walk on the beach, Clara." He turned a flashlight on, which threw a yellow circle of light on the sand at his bare feet. "I'm sure our driver won't mind if I borrow the flashlight he left in our room."

"We've not had our walk yet," Noah said, a hint of aggravation in his voice. "Regardless, I'll let you two go ahead."

As he left down the path for the hotel, Vernon watched him. "I can't place my finger on it, but there's something about him I don't like." He faced Clara, eyes narrowing in the light of the single bulb in the gazebo. "It's almost as if you two were more than friends in the past. That isn't true, is it? Your mother and father seemed awfully fond of him when they recommended I hire him to drive us here."

Clara hated to lie, but she felt as if she didn't have a choice. If not, Vernon might call off their courtship, and she wouldn't be fulfilling her goal of being the proper Beachy Amish Mennonite wife and mother.

Vernon held out his hand. "We're hardly teenagers, Clara. Can we please hold hands on our first walk on the beach?"

Hand in hand they eased down the sandy dune. A time or two Clara slipped in the sand, and Vernon steadied her. "Whoa, now, young lady. I'd hate to have us fall and get sand where sand isn't supposed to be. That would be mighty uncomfortable, wouldn't it?"

Having never heard his humorous side before, she couldn't help but giggle. "Oh, I agree," she said, stopping to wiggle her toes in the sand. "The last time John played in the garden with his toy truck, he came in complaining about dirt in his pants. Edna and I couldn't help laughing at how he was walking with his legs spread."

Vernon chuckled softly. "You've raised two wonderful children. I know Abram is proud."

He led her to where the waves broke on the sand, spreading like a lace tablecloth. Every few steps she squealed at a crab as it scurried into a hole, and Vernon chuckled again. Although he said they were called ghost crabs, and they were more scared of her than she was of them, the way they darted left and right on their spike-like legs still made her think it might hurt if they ran across her toes.

They stopped on the edge of the lace tablecloth. Clara raised the hem of her dress to her knees to keep the surf from wetting it. The flashlight beam darted across her calves. She hadn't thought Vernon, her stern and stoic bishop, would do such a thing as catching a glimpse of her legs. Although he was a Beachy Amish man, he was still a man, like King David when he admired lovely Bathsheba bathing on her rooftop.

Vernon chuckled once more, his face barely

visible in the starlight. Clara hadn't noticed the absence of his hat. Without it, he looked boyish, even cute in a way. "What are you laughing at?" she asked.

"It's the English and how they think we Amish and Mennonites never sin. We're human like them, so of course we sin. Take myself for instance—I've done things I regret, things I've prayed to God for forgiveness for." He flashed the light across her calves again. "Like admiring your beauty. I hope you forgive me."

His tone carried a hint of melancholy, as if more serious sins hid in his past, possibly having to do with his wife. Clara doubted it. He wouldn't lie about something as important as his wife's death.

Touched by his admitting to admiring her legs, she gently squeezed his arm. "There's nothing to forgive. We're all sinners. What's important is searching our hearts for what makes us sin so we don't do it again."

Vernon looked up into the heavens. "All those stars, and I managed to find the brightest one on a farm in southern Virginia." He faced Clara again, his white teeth showing with a soft smile. "Imagine that." He took her hand and led her along the beach, their feet splashing in the surf, her still holding up the hem of her dress.

Completely stunned by Vernon calling her the

brightest star, Clara had no idea he could be so romantic. Like she had asked herself before, could he actually be a man she could fall in love with, maybe even more than how she loved Jonah now?

In the eastern sky, a meteor left a crimson trail, then winked out as if it had never existed. She had seen the same thing once as a child, when she and Papa sat outside on the porch at the end of a long summer day. She said it looked like a sign of something good happening. He shook his head and frowned, eyes visible in the light overhead. "Not at all, Clara, not at all. The night before my grandmother died, I saw that same thing. Ever since then it's been a sign of sadness to come. If you see a star burn like that, say your prayers, because something terrible is going to happen."

From across the ocean, a cold breeze chilled her as if an evil presence were whispering: *Beware, Clara. I took your beloved Abram and almost took Edna with that spider's poison. Now I'm ready to take someone else you care for, and you can't do a thing to stop it.*

She shivered at the sudden cold and the sense of foreboding. Vernon stopped. "You're shaking, are you cold?"

Clara lay her head on his chest. He wrapped his arms around her. Although his warmth stopped her from shivering, it failed to ease her fear of losing someone she loved, whoever that might be. Could either Papa or Mama be sick, or perhaps Alfred or Susan, her brother and sister?

Vernon's chest shuddered. "Clara," he sobbed. "Do you know how happy you make me? When I lost my wife, I never thought I'd be happy again."

She squeezed him tight. "Shh, don't cry. I'm sure she wants the best for you."

"And you *are* the best." He pulled away. "All right, enough of that nonsense, a grown man crying like a child. What would you like to do tomorrow? We still have five more days before we leave this coming Saturday."

"I really don't know. You know more about what to do here than I do."

"I'd say we could see the Lost Colony play on Manteo, but the season ended in August." He snapped his fingers. "We could go fishing on one of the piers. You know how I like fish."

Clara said nothing. She still remembered how Vernon had scolded Edna when Jonah had taken them fishing last year, when she threw the one fish they caught back in the lake.

"Well," Vernon said, "maybe you'd rather not have your hands smell like bait. We could climb Jockey's Ridge to watch the sunset one afternoon. They're the largest sand dunes on the east coast, with a wonderful view of the sound. There's also the Manteo Waterfront. It has lots of restaurants and shops, and a nice bookstore called Downtown Books. We could visit the Elizabethan Gardens too. They have a butterfly garden and a path that winds along the sound."

Clara looked up at him, his face barely visible in the starlight. "How do you know about all those places? It's like you've been here before." She didn't add what she was thinking: *Like you've been here before—with your wife.* What else didn't she know about him? As she waited for his answer, he looked up at the stars.

"What a beautiful site God has made." He covered a yawn. "We'll decide what to do in in the morning." Turning her by the arm, he let go, as if something from his past had made him turn away, either from her or the truth between him and his wife.

At the bottom of the path from the gazebo, they brushed sand from their feet before stepping onto the sidewalk leading to the hotel. Without so much as a "good night," Vernon left for his room. Noting how he had avoided answering the question of how he knew so much about this area, Clara went to her room also.

After a shower, she climbed into bed and checked her phone for calls or texts. Two texts from

John and Edna using Alison's phone said they were fine. Both asked her to bring some sea shells home. Alison asked how the courting was going and if Noah was behaving. That's what Clara got for confiding in her best friend not long after they had met; some secrets could come back to haunt a person.

Seeing no texts from Jonah about his work on the kitchen, she hovered her fingertip over his number. Text him or not? Call him or not? She would love to hear his voice. He got so excited when he spoke of his electrical work or tending his beef cattle, he sounded like a little boy with a new toy. With such a work ethic, he would be a valued member of her community if he were to join. The ladies had certainly enjoyed their talk with him the last time they met for church at Alison's home, when Vernon was out of town and the men were sick. He had even won over Mrs. Yoder, who normally couldn't abide English ways.

Clara returned the phone to the nightstand and took the quartz stone, still in its matchbox, from the drawer. The lamplight reflected off the surface, glassy and heart shaped, calling to her. She pressed it to her cheek, mimicking the touch of cool lips. When Jonah had given it to her during their talk on the shores of the lake in Occoneechee State Park, saying he would treasure it if she kept it for him, the gesture—plus his words—had filled her with longing. What about him made her love him so much? It was more than all the things he had done for her: plowing the garden not long after Abram died and before she had learned to drive the tractor; saving Edna's life by speeding them to the hospital when the Black Widow spider bit her; possibly paying for the hospital bill with a Go Fund Me account; insisting the entire family stay with him and Lydia until Clara could care for herself and the children after her miscarriage; giving her the phone she now used; possibly giving her the propane stove she loved; wiring the kitchen for electricity. Yes, all those things were wonderful, but it was more than that, such as when they went on their drive in Pennsylvania last year, when he had held her in his lap and told her she would have to decide the choices in her life.

The red braid lay across Clara's shoulder. She tickled her nose with it. On their drive that night, she hadn't bothered to wear a kapp, having gotten ready for bed. Unafraid, Jonah wrapped his arms around her as if she were a troubled child, offering the wisdom of his advice. Yes, no one but her could choose the direction of her life, but she wished the road she traveled—and her choice—would take her to him.

She kissed the stone and returned it to the nightstand drawer. But now her road led to Vernon. On the day he asked her to marry him, she would drive to Occoneechee State Park and leave the tiny piece of quartz on the shore where Jonah had found it, closing the door on the possibility of marrying him forever.

* * *

Walking the starlit beach without his flashlight because Vernon had drained the batteries, Noah kicked sand and shells aside. No one had called about any improprieties concerning Vernon's wife or her death, but something was amiss. One thing was Vernon's recent three-week trip, all of it unaccounted for. Another was how no one knew what community he was originally from. Yet another was a rumor about him attending a funeral during his trip. Not only was the woman's name a mystery, the names of his parents were too.

Returning to the hotel, he stopped to watch the light coming from the rear window of Clara's room. Just the thought of Vernon marrying her sickened him. She deserved a younger man. She deserved someone who truly loved her. She deserved a man who would cherish her all the days of her life, including her children, John and Edna.

In his pocket, his cell phone vibrated. The screen showed a text from one of his friends checking into

Vernon. He had tracked the old bishop's home state to Indiana, but not his hometown. Also, Vernon's wife was named Nell, and she was from Indiana too.

Not ready to go inside yet, Noah trudged up the wooden walkway past the gazebo and slid down the dune on the other side on his way back to the beach. Walking in the edge of the cool surf, he started texting a reply when a wave come up to his knees. As it hissed back out, it sucked the sand from beneath his feet, making him lose his balance and fall, soaking the cell phone in salt water in the process. The screen blinked several times and went out. Noah was tempted to throw it in the ocean, but he had heard of putting a cell phone in a plastic bag filled with rice to remove the moisture from it.

He trudged up this side of the dune. The feeling that he was about to learn something to end Vernon's pursuit of Clara aggravated him even worse than his wet phone. Leaving wet footprints in the hotel parking lot and along the sidewalk, he hurried along until he arrived at the store where he bought the ice cream. Inside, he bought two bags of rice and a box of plastic storage bags with zip closures, ignoring the cashier's stare at his wet pants up to the knees and his sandy feet.

Outside, he dumped one bag of rice into a

storage bag, put the phone in, and dumped the second bag in, then zipped the enclosure. With the empty rice bags and the remainder of the storage bags in a nearby trash can, he hurried back to the hotel holding the rice-filled storage bag to his chest as if it contained the key to Clara's heart.

The plastic card opened the room door with a soft click. He tiptoed past the first bed, where Vernon snored. After storing the bag in his suitcase, he showered the sand off his feet, dressed in pajamas, and climbed into bed.

One way or another, even if Noah had to drive all the way to Indiana himself to discover the truth about Nell, Clara would never have to hear old man Vernon's window-rattling snores. First, he hoped the cell phone would work, and the sooner the better.

Chapter 13

On Friday, her last full day on the Outer Banks, Clara sat with a bowl of cereal in the hotel's continental breakfast area. She had enjoyed the last few days. Tuesday, Vernon had driven her to the Elizabethan Gardens in the town of Manteo, across the two bridges that connected Nags Head to Roanoke Island. They had walked hand in hand amongst huge oaks, their limbs twisted as if a tornado had ravaged them and left them that way to show the direction of the prevailing winds. Near the visitor's center, flowers of all kinds attracted butterflies of all kinds. Not far from the beginning of the path they had walked, a statue of Virginia Dare, the first English child born in the New World, reminded Clara of the hardships the first colony to this area had suffered. Its namesake play, The Lost Colony, according to a brochure in the visitor's center, told how all the colonists had vanished while John White, Virginia's grandfather, had returned to England for supplies.

Wednesday, it had rained until after an early

supper, so they had stayed in their rooms. As the showers slowed to cool mist, Vernon suggested they take advantage of the comfortable temperature to climb Jockey's Ridge. Like he had said, the view of the sunset had been perfect, colored with layer upon layer of oranges, purples, scarlets and every color in between, as if God himself had painted the clouds over the horizon with His majestic fingertip.

Thursday, before breakfast, Noah said he needed to find a cell phone shop because his wasn't working. Both Clara and Vernon offered theirs but he turned them down, saying he preferred his. He returned from his search, complaining that no one could fix it, so he had to buy a new one. After they ate in the continental breakfast area, he suggested they visit the Bodie Island Lighthouse. Vernon suggested the Cape Hatteras Lighthouse instead. The drive down Highway 12 and back, plus the climb to the top, took most of the day, but it had been worth it. The view of the slender strand of sand and woods called the Outer Banks, from the walkway almost 200 hundred feet tall, had been amazing, as if she were an osprey from the lake back home, soaring above it all. On the drive back, as they passed the Bodie Island Lighthouse, which was much closer to Nags Head, Clara wondered why Vernon had suggested the much longer drive to Hatteras. Regardless, it was a day she would never forget.

Also during their time together, Vernon had grown more affectionate and caring, asking if she was having a good time, if she was thirsty or hungry, even offering to buy gifts for John and Edna at one of the many tourist shops from Kitty Hawk to Nags Head. The more time Clara spent with him, even though Noah hovered nearby like a hawk, the more she thought she might come to love him one day.

Done with the cereal, Clara threw the paper bowl away and chose coffee and a pastry. As she sat, Noah came in, chose oatmeal, and joined her. "I sure miss eggs and bacon and biscuits."

Clara had heard his complaint before. Since Vernon said he was paying for everything, Noah hadn't brought much money, so he couldn't go out for breakfast like he wanted. Time to change the subject. "How's your new phone working?"

Noah blew a frustrated breath. "The store couldn't transfer my numbers to the new one. I remember a few of them, but not many. I have them written down at home."

"Are you expecting any important calls? People can still call you if you are."

About to take a bite of oatmeal, Noah lowered

the spoon. "I realize that. I prefer to have all the numbers in this new phone now."

Returning to her breakfast, Clara wondered what was so important about him having every single number in his phone now instead of when he got home.

Vernon came in and nodded at her, poured coffee, filled a bowl with scrambled eggs, and joined them at the table. "These eggs are fine, but I'd rather have them over easy."

Noah eyed him. "Then let's go to a restaurant. We haven't been to one all week for breakfast."

Vernon eyed him back. "Didn't you see the prices in the menus when we went for supper?"

"I understand being frugal, Vernon, but if I had known you weren't going to pay for breakfast, I would've brought more money of my own. I'm sure Clara is tired of eating the same old thing every day too."

Saying nothing, Vernon ate his eggs and drank coffee. Done with both, he threw the paper bowl and cup away and returned to his seat. "Clara, part of the reason I've been saving my money is for a surprise for you." He glared at Noah. "And it doesn't include grumpy drivers."

Noah looked up from his second bowl of oatmeal. "You're not taking my car and leaving me like you did when you took Clara to those gardens and to those sand dunes. I got bored sitting around here all day."

"That's true," Clara said to Vernon. "It wasn't fair to do that to Noah."

Vernon gave his head a slight shake. "Oh, he can drive us, but he can't do what we're going to do." He stood. "Let's go. I've got something I want to show you."

* * *

Driving south down Highway 12, where Vernon had said to go, Noah squeezed the steering wheel as if he wanted to twist the vinyl cover off. The phone number of his most important informant concerning the old man's wife was right on the tip of his tongue, and he wanted to call to see if he had any more news. Up ahead to the right, the Bodie Island Lighthouse appeared from above the crowns of those twisted trees so prevalent in this area. Vernon said to take a right toward the lighthouse, so Noah turned in. He wanted to complain that they could have gone here instead of driving all the way to Hatteras the other day but knew it would do no good. Like a spoiled child who needed a spanking, old man Vernon had to have his way. If Noah had anything to do with it, and he did, the facts surrounding Vernon's wife would soon give him a spanking, as well as make Clara see the light concerning his lies.

When they neared the lighthouse, which resembled a stack of black and white doughnuts growing smaller in diameter as they reached the top, Vernon said to park. He peered left and right. "I don't understand. The website said they would be on this road."

"Who's they?" Noah grumbled. "Why all the secrecy?"

"It's a surprise, like I already told you."

Noah snorted laughter. "Huh. It looks like the surprise is on you."

"Now, now," Clara said from the back seat. "Let's not be rude."

"Go back out to the main road," Vernon said. When Noah did, Vernon pointed out the windshield. "There they are."

"All I see is a horse trailer." Noah said.

Clara clapped her hands. "I know what the surprise is, Vernon. You showed me a brochure about it. We're going to ride horses on the beach."

"That trailer has three horses in it," Noah said to Vernon. "I thought I had to stay here."

"The other horse is for our guide," Vernon said, patting Noah's shoulder. "You get to stay here and smell what those three horses left in that trailer."

Noah cut his eyes at Vernon. "Not if I know what time to come back. How long does the ride last?"

A young woman climbed from the pickup attached to the trailer and came to Noah's car. He rolled the window down, and she asked if they were her clients.

"Me and the lady in back are," Vernon said. "This donkey with us is just our driver."

Getting out of the car, Clara giggled. "See you later, donkey. Maybe you can find another donkey to hee-haw with while we're gone."

The young woman saddled the horses and took a box from the pickup to give Clara and Vernon a boost when they climbed into their saddles. Clara had to bring her dress up past her knees to sit properly, and Noah's cheeks heated upon seeing her long legs. She waved at him, and his heart skipped a beat. Several strands of hair had fallen from her kapp, giving her a wild and free appearance. She smiled like a child on Christmas morning, and he wished he could be the man riding with her on the beach instead of old Vernon.

In the saddle now, the guide waved them toward a path to the beach, where they took a right. The tall sand dune, topped with what Noah had learned were sea oats, soon blocked his view.

Squeezing the steering wheel like he had earlier, he was tempted to run after them. Instead, he took his phone from his pocket and frowned at the screen. Why hadn't anyone of his informants called or texted? And why couldn't he remember the number of the man who had texted about the funeral Vernon had recently attended? And who was the funeral for?

* * *

Riding to Clara's left, the guide, Sharon, looked her way. "You're a natural on a horse. When I asked you and your partner about your experience with horses, I thought you both might have some, being Amish."

To Clara's right, Vernon laughed. "Mine was on a pony. It's a lot farther to fall from a horse."

They were riding halfway between the surf and the dunes. Here and there, fisherman and women had parked both pickups and jeeps, with rods in racks on the front bumpers. Most also had huge coolers on platforms attached to the bumpers. These people took their fishing seriously.

Sharon wore shorts, a T-shirt, and sandals. Her brunette hair in a long ponytail bounced back and forth along her shoulders in time with the horse's gait.

The mid-September sun soon rose high enough to set beads of sweat on Clara's forehead. She longed to remove the kapp and unpin her hair to let the ocean breeze blow through it. If she had been alone, or maybe with Jonah, she might do that very thing. With her stoic bishop, Vernon, she thought better of it.

Although he wore a wide-brimmed straw hat to shade his face, sweat soon beaded his brow as well. His black pants weren't helping matters, evidenced by how he rubbed his thighs as if they were hot. He removed the hat and wiped his forehead with his sleeve. "Whew, maybe we should've come down here in October."

"That's a nice time of the year," Sharon said, except we end the tours at the end of September.

As they rode along, Clara still longed to remove her kapp. She knew it was wrong, knew it might upset Vernon, but she wanted to experience the ride the same as Sharon: wild and free and unfettered by so much clothing, such as the dress smothering her legs. She faced Vernon. "I hate to ask but I'm hot too. Do you mind if I take off my kapp and unpin my hair? It's only you and me, so shouldn't it be all right?"

Vernon answered with a smile. "I don't mind, but a lot of those Englishers who think the Amish wouldn't dare break any of our rules might mind. Go ahead. I won't tell."

The kapp came off quickly, followed by the pins. Clara's red hair trundled down her shoulders and back as she shook it free, smiling at Vernon. He placed his hand to his chest. "Clara, you are so lovely, it makes my heart hurt."

She faced Sharon. "Can we go faster? I want to see what it felt like to be a wild woman from back in the old western days."

Grinning, Sharon heeled her horse. As sand flew from its hooves, Clara heeled her horse too. "Yah!" she yelled. Yes, this was freedom: the pounding of hooves in the sand, the press of the stirrups against the soles of her tennis shoes, her dress flaring around her thighs, her bottom bouncing in the saddle, the leather reins in her hands, the wind in her hair, the smell of salt air a reminder of the sea. If Mama and Papa saw her now, they would either faint or threaten to shun her.

She turned her head to look for Vernon, but he was still sitting where she had left him, teeth white in the sunlight. He threw up a hand and waved, the happiest she had ever seen him.

For the Amish and Mennonites, Clara knows, freedom takes many forms. One is the freedom to worship God through their interpretation of the Bible. Another is their love of family and community. Yet another is living as one with nature, raising and gathering their food, both from animals and gardens. Still another might be breaking a small rule here and there to release themselves from their strict Ordnungs, knowing all the while how God understands the human heart and its need to—in the case of something as simple as riding a horse—become one with the wonderful world He created for everyone, whether they are Amish or Mennonite or not.

Sharon wheeled her horse and trotted it back toward Vernon, who had dismounted. Clara followed, regretting the end of her moment of freedom. As she neared him, he clapped his hands. "What a site you were, Clara. I was both thrilled and scared. I could've sworn you were going to fall off."

She brought her right leg over the saddle and slid down next to Vernon, then looked up at him, the thrill of the ride still coursing through her veins. "Well now, if you had sworn, both of us would've broken our Ordnung today." She wrapped her arms around his neck and pulled him down. "Let's break it one more time with a kiss."

* * *

At the path to the beach, despite Clara and Vernon's kiss, Noah pumped his fist. He had just gotten a text from his main informer. When Clara knew the truth about Vernon's lies, she would rather slap his face than kiss him.

He hurried back to the car.

But he would wait to tell her at the end of their

trip. If not, they might have to leave Vernon in Nags Head, or the entire ride back to her house would be filled with misery.

Noah cranked the car and turned the air conditioning on. He didn't like stirring up all this trouble, nor the pain it would cause Clara, but the truth needed to be known. Before long, Vernon would regret his lies. What he better do is fall on his knees and ask God for forgiveness, because no air conditioning ever invented would cool him from the fires of hell. Still, Noah regretted this situation. For a Beachy Amish bishop to fail so badly, he might've had a reason. Regardless, Noah intended to comfort Clara, and hopefully, to win her love like she had won his so long ago.

Chapter 14

On the way home, Vernon had thoughtfully asked Noah to pick John and Edna up from Alison's. Clara thanked her for keeping them, said she hoped they weren't too much trouble, and said she would be happy to repay the favor anytime.

On the porch, Alison smiled. "They weren't the least bit of trouble. In fact, they kept my boys out from under my feet and out in the yard playing most of the time."

Samuel had called Vernon and Noah over to ask about a problem with his tractor parked nearby. Alison took Clara by the arm and led her across the porch away from them. "Did you enjoy your trip? Does Vernon have a romantic streak we've never seen?"

Turning away to avoid betraying her conspiratorial grin to the men, Clara shook her head. "You and your romantic notions. You know marriage is more for family and community than it is for romance."

"Phooey on you, Clara Engelman. Like you

didn't marry Abram for love."

"Phooey right back at you. You said romance. There's a difference between love and romance, as you well know." Clara paused. What would be the harm in at least telling her best friend about the horse ride?

As the men continued to talk about the tractor, then about the hog butchering season to come, and as the children took turns in a swing hanging from a huge oak on the opposite side of the yard, Clara told Alison each and every detail about her horse ride with Vernon, leaving out the one kiss, of course.

"My goodness," Alison said, widening her eyes. "I wish Samuel would take me on a romantic horseback ride on the beach." She looked toward the men and returned to Clara. "How did things go with Noah? Having your old beau along while Vernon courted you must've been interesting."

"I haven't told Vernon about my past with Noah, so keep it to yourself." Clara glanced at the men too. "It was strange at first. Every chance Noah got, he told me Vernon was too old or some other reason to not court him. Then, about halfway into the trip, he stopped saying anything like that. Maybe he's given up on us being together again." Clara hesitated. She wondered how Jonah was doing, especially if he had seen Tess outside of their guitar lessons. "Did ... well, how much work has Jonah done on my kitchen?"

Alison rolled her eyes. "Listen to you, wanting to know how much time Jonah has been spending with Tess instead of working on the wiring. Anyone with eyes knows you're attracted to him. Even Lydia has seen it."

Clara pushed her lips in and out, her bad habit of an impatient pout. "That's not answering my question."

Leaning close to Clara's ear, Alison whispered, "Jonah and Tess have seen each other three times this week alone. He's working on your kitchen today because he got behind." Alison shoved Clara's arm. "Go on, be honest. Don't you have feelings for him? Like I already told you, maybe you can talk him into joining our community. If Vernon ever left, he'd make a fine bishop. The ladies really enjoyed talking with him that day at my house."

Over by the tractor, Vernon and Samuel laughed at something while Noah looked on, his features tense. He glanced at Clara, clenched his fists at his sides, and turned away.

What in the world is wrong with him? Clara wondered.

Alison shoved her arm again. "You're not

listening to me."

Clara faced her. "I ... I was wondering how much Jonah has done on the kitchen. What did you say?"

"I was telling you how Lydia and I went shopping in Clarksville at Hite's clothing store. She talked me into buying a nighty to tempt Samuel for our anniversary next month."

"It sounds like you and Lydia have become good friends." Clara didn't say the rest: *so maybe you can find out if she's Jonah's sister or not, and what happened to her arm to make it crooked at the elbow, plus that scar she has.*

"Oh, yes," Alison continued. "Lydia and I are *very* good friends."

Vernon and Samuel came over. Noah got in the car and slammed the door, his cheeks blood red. "I should get you and the children home," Vernon said. "I'm sure you want to see how Jonah's coming with the wiring."

Clara thanked Alison again for keeping the children, including Samuel this time. With John and Edna's suitcases in the trunk and them beside her in the back seat of the car, Noah silently drove away.

In the front seat, Vernon twisted around to face her. "It sure is good to be back in Virginia. No matter where I've lived, I enjoy Virginia the best."

"Is that so?" Noah blurted. "Just how many places have you lived? I've heard it's quite a few."

"I've moved a lot since my wife died. What of it?"

"Oh, just rumors."

Clara watched Vernon turn around. The muscles in his neck tightened with a hard swallow. Surely he wasn't hiding anything about his wife. If so, especially if he was lying, she needed to know now, just as her feelings for him were growing.

Thirty minutes later, Noah parked behind Jonah's pickup truck. Walking to the tailgate with a roll of wire, he had taken his shirt off. Sweat glistened on his chest. His muscles flexed as he lay the roll of wire in the truck's bed and put his shirt on, taken from where it was draped over the side of the pickup bed. It was all Clara could do to not gape at his statuesque form.

"Look at him," Noah said. "What kind of man stands around half naked like that?"

"A very *hot* man," Clara said, regretting the double meaning of her statement. Yet again, she would have to pray to God, this time to forgive her attraction to Jonah's manly body.

Vernon got out and took the children's luggage to the porch and came back for Clara's suitcase. Done with that, he clapped Jonah on the back.

"How goes the wiring, Jonah? We might have a wedding soon, and Clara and I will need electricity in at least the kitchen."

Noah let the children out. They ran inside, likely to see Jonah's work. He then strode over to Vernon. "You and Clara just started courting. I wouldn't count my chickens before they hatch. One might get eaten by a wily fox waiting for a meal."

Vernon eyed Noah. "You're very talkative after being quiet the last few days. If you have something to say, just say it."

Jonah's eyebrows arched higher than Clara had ever seen them. "Maybe you two are tired after that long drive," he said. "I know I would be." He faced Clara. "Let me show you the kitchen. Then you can rest. I'm sure you're tired too."

"That's a good idea," Noah said. He faced Clara. "I'm going to stay in a hotel tonight in South Boston. I'd like to see the kitchen in the morning if you don't mind." He led Vernon away by the elbow. "Let's get you home. Jonah's right and I apologize. I'm tired from the drive and it's made me grouchy."

Vernon went with him. "I'm glad you see your error, Noah. I apologize for snapping at you as well."

Clara watched them drive away, feeling as if she'd just stepped from the eye of an Outer Banks hurricane about to bear down on them all. She followed Jonah into the kitchen, where she crossed her hands over her chest. "Jonah, you shouldn't have. A new refrigerator and a washer?"

"Yay!" Edna shrieked, running in from the hall. "No more wringing water out of my dresses!"

John opened the refrigerator and took out a bottle of water. "Thank you, Jonah. Water's a lot better cold than hot."

"Speaking of hot water," Jonah said, going to the sink to lift the faucet lever, "come here and feel this, Clara."

She did so. At first the water was cool; then it gradually warmed until it was hot. She faced Jonah. "You installed a hot water heater too?"

"I sure did. I worked all last night and today to finish everything. I want to do the rest of the house before winter. I hope you like what's ready now."

Clara didn't know what to say, so she said the first thing that popped into her mind. "You are so sweet, Jonah Ellis."

He laughed. "You won't say that when you see the bill. If it helps, you can pay by the month."

"How do I know if you're teasing or not?"

"By my laughing. Consider the washer and refrigerator and hot water heater wedding gifts. Lydia wanted a new refrigerator and washer anyway, so I installed ours here." He looked away and back, lips working in and out like a man with something on his mind. "I hope you enjoyed your time at the beach."

Clara noticed he didn't say he hoped she enjoyed her time at the beach with Vernon. "It was nice," she said, aware that the excitement of the horse ride had worn off. Tell him about it or not? "We did a lot of beachy things. That was about it."

"So you enjoyed it, I'm glad. All I want is for you to be happy."

From down the hall, John and Edna's voices murmured quietly, likely talking about their time at Alison's.

Clara looked up into Jonah's eyes. The cleft in his chin, the dark growth of today's whiskers, his strong nose and square jaw. Still, he was more than his physical appearance; he was a comforter and a friend, like that night in Pennsylvania when he had held her in his lap like a sad child. Darkness fell around them, until they were the only two people in the world. Thunder pulsed in her chest: a runaway heartbeat like horse's hooves pounding the sand. Jonah smiled softly and she did too, and she fell in love with him all over again. If only the world could be shoved away, including Vernon and Noah and everyone and everything in it. No sin, no judgement—no Amish, no English—only a love as pure and true and wonderful as the love she felt for this amazing man standing before her. She wanted him in every way possible, to have his children, to share his life. Was it wrong to feel so deeply for a man outside the strict rules of the Ordnung, even to the point of being shunned if she left her community?

The darkness brightened. The thunder quieted. Within her chest, the horse's hooves slowed to a trot. Yes, all of what she had just felt and thought was wrong. She must follow her Ordnung, must beg God's forgiveness. How many times must she admonish herself for her sins before she stopped committing them?

Clara slipped her hand in her pocket. The matchbox with the heart-shaped stone Jonah had given her rested there. She should drive to Occoneechee State Park and throw it into the lake tonight, but it would be like throwing away a part of her soul.

Jonah leaned down to gaze into her eyes. "Are you okay?"

Clara dropped into a chair at the table. "I … Yes, I'm tired. Like you said, it was a long drive."

Jonah remained standing. "You must've forgotten to ask anyone to feed the chickens and gather eggs and feed and milk the cow. Lydia helped with all that while you were gone." He opened the refrigerator and grinned. "I hope you like milk and eggs, you've got plenty of both." He took out a carton of eggs. "It's almost suppertime. Lydia's visiting her mother, so I could make you and the children something to eat." He took out cheese and tomatoes and spinach. "How about an omelet? I love a good omelet."

Clara's head was down. She didn't dare raise it to ask why he was so good to her. To him they were just friends, just neighbors, nothing more and nothing less.

She told him not to worry about her and the children, told him thank you again for his work, told him she would work out payments for it, told him he could go, told him he must be tired too.

When the door closed behind him, she went out on the porch and wrapped her arms around herself as she watched him drive away.

Footsteps pattered behind her. The door opened. John took one hand, Edna the other. They also watched the pickup head down the road toward his driveway.

"Why didn't Jonah stay," Edna asked. "I missed him."

"Me too," John said.

Without answering, Clara took them back inside to make omelets. When they were done eating, she bathed them in the tub, enjoying how she didn't have to heat water on the propane stove someone had surprised her with last year. Jonah and Vernon denied any part in it, but Jonah must've given it to her, like he had given her so much else.

After getting John and Edna in bed, Clara took a flashlight to Abram's grave, its beam lighting the path to the oak tree in the back yard. She turned the light off and waited for her eyes to adjust to the darkness. Gasping in shame, she dropped to her knees in the grass, wet with dew. All her life she had been taught to follow the light of God's word, but would she have to adjust to the darkness of the English world to marry the one man she truly loved, who no one, not even sweet Vernon or caring Noah could replace?

She pressed her cheek against the wooden cross. "Heavenly Father," she whispered, her voice edged in tears, "please forgive me. My heart is heavy with wickedness and sin from loving a man who lives in the English world instead of in my world." She paused to suck in a ragged breath, hot tears streaming down her cheeks. "But how can my love for a man as good and kind as Jonah be sinful and wicked just because he's not like Beachy Amish Mennonite? The Bible says You made us all in your image, so aren't we all worthy of love?"

Clara raised her head. Over the grassy hill separating her and Jonah's homes, a light shown from his bedroom window. A shadow moved across the curtain, barely visible from this distance, or perhaps she was imagining it.

Her knees were soaked from the dew. The September night chilled her, making her shiver. Still, the freshness of the air, crisp and cool, filled her with hope. Regardless, what hope did she have of being with Jonah? Her only hope of honoring God and her Beachy Amish Mennonite Ordnung was to marry Vernon, a man she knew she would never love like she loved Abram and Jonah.

In the house again, after getting ready for bed, she placed the matchbox with the heart shaped stone beneath her pillow. Standing beside the nightstand, where the kerosene lamp threw a pool of light, flickering and yellow, around the room, she ran her fingertips across the pillow as if it were either Abram's or Jonah's face.

Then another face lingered there—not Vernon's—but a face from her youth. Despite her earlier statement about not being able to love Noah, was it possible? She had once felt something akin to love for him when they were teenagers, so perhaps she could find that feeling again. This thing with Vernon wouldn't work in the long run. She had kissed him to see if he could set the spark of love flaming within her, but it had only left the empty embrace of an icy winter wind howling around the corners of her mind.

On her knees, she clasped her hands together. Not closing her eyes, she realized Jonah hadn't shown her the light switches in the kitchen, although she remembered seeing them. Still, it would've been amazing to do something as simple as flipping a switch and illuminating the room she spent so much time in.

She rose and went to the kitchen, flipped a switch for a flash of brilliance, and flipped it off again.

There, like that single burst of light, maybe, possibly, though highly unlikely, she had extinguished her feelings for the one man in the world who could make her as happy as Abram had.

And maybe more.

Chapter 15

Sitting on the end of the hotel bed, Noah put the fast-food sausage and egg biscuit back in the bag. He had managed a hamburger and a bottle of water last night for supper, but after only one bite of the biscuit, his stomach knotted with fear from having to tell Clara about Vernon's lies concerning his wife. Not only that, he hadn't slept well, rolling over to glare at the nightstand clock's green LED numbers every few minutes. Toward dawn, when the rising sun colored the curtains red, he had managed to sleep about an hour. Now, as if the wind at the Outer Banks had blown sand in his eyes, the grit of so little sleep aggravated him near to madness.

He took the Styrofoam cup from the nightstand and sipped. At least he could drink coffee, which was quite good for a fast-food place.

Before bed he had prayed and prayed, his initial anger at Vernon having dissipated. He felt sorry for him more than anything now, felt sorry for how the news would affect him, felt sorry especially for how it would affect Clara. That kiss on the beach meant she cared about him. His lies meant he might have to resign from being a bishop, at least from his small community north of Nathalie. They would likely forgive him if he admitted all and repented. It would be up to them if it came to it. Then again, Noah had never heard of a situation like this. Beachy Amish men had sinned before. If they repented, they could be forgiven to keep from tearing a community apart and to promote harmony. Unfortunately for Vernon, his sins were some of the worst Noah had heard of.

He finished the coffee and called his contact to make absolutely sure of all the facts, then packed his suitcase and climbed into his car for the drive to Clara's.

Lord, forgive me, he prayed. *I don't begrudge Vernon any happiness, and I certainly don't begrudge Clara any happiness either. That's all I've ever wanted for her—nothing more, nothing less. Amen.*

The white lines in the road flew by. Nausea at the coming scene roiled his gut, causing him to burp coffee into his throat. He had never been so nervous and upset in his life. Even when Clara told him she was going to court Abram, along with their engagement a year later, he hadn't been this upset. The look in her eyes when she spoke of Abram told of her love for him, and his love for her had made

Noah smile at the prospect of her happiness, even giving him hope of finding happiness too.

But it wasn't meant to be.

Whenever he looked into another woman's eyes, he only saw the lovely green eyes of Clara looking back. It was the same with holding another hand, with carrying on a conversation, with a walk after a singing.

He took a right off the main highway. Minutes later, nearing Clara's home, he hit the brakes so hard the tires squawked to a stop.

Vernon's car sat in the driveway, and he and Clara stood inside the barn door, each staring his way.

He eased into the driveway, sweat chilling his forehead despite the cool morning air blowing from the car's vents. If only this weight could be lifted from his shoulders, but lies and dishonesty could destroy a community, and this one was small enough to start with.

He parked between Vernon's car and the house to allow the bishop a short walk when he left, as he surely would leave once Clara heard the truth.

Closing the car door, Noah placed his wide-brimmed hat made of black felt on his head. Steps later, he stood just inside the barn door.

"That's right," Clara said to him. "You wanted to see Jonah's work this morning. Have you eaten breakfast? The children are still asleep, so I was going to surprise them with pancakes."

Vernon tipped a black leather hat, possibly his Sunday hat, possibly his most impressive hat to wear while asking Clara to marry him.

Nausea boiled up into Noah's throat again. "Clara, I don't know how to say this, but Vernon's not who you think he is. His wife only died recently. That's why he went on that trip, to attend to her legal matters and to bury her. He's lied to numerous people over the last ten years about her. She had a nervous breakdown shortly after they married. He left her with her parents and started moving from community to community to make a new life for himself. All that time he lied over and over again about his past. Her illness worsened so much she killed herself. I'm sorry. The last thing I want is to cause you pain."

Clara's knees buckled. Noah caught her. Vernon said nothing, did nothing, showed not one bit of emotion in his blank expression. Noah eased Clara onto a three-legged milking stool nearby and asked if he could get her some water.

Her pale face regained some of its color. She glared up at Vernon. "Is any of that true? It's … I don't have the words for how terrible it is. You left your wife because she had a nervous breakdown?

Then you lied to anyone who would listen after that? How could you be so deceitful? You, a Beachy Amish Mennonite bishop?"

Vernon's nostrils flared. His face reddened to a ruddy red, like the muddy Dan River in South Boston after several days of rain. The color drained from his face, and he dropped to his backside into the thin layer of hay covering the barn's dirt floor. His head fell forward. Terrible sobs shook his shoulders until he hiccupped as if he would choke to death. Tears from his eyes and mucous from his nose dripped into his lap. Noah truly regretted this moment. The man was broken, beaten, the weight of his sins pressing on him hard enough to rip his soul from his body.

Clara worked herself up, pulling at Noah's arms until she stood upright. She said nothing, simply shook her head at the sadness of the situation.

Noah gently took her by the arms and turned her toward him and away from Vernon. "Clara, ever since I started caring for you when we were young, all I've ever wanted is for you to be happy. If you love Vernon and want to marry him, I'll leave and never tell anyone about this."

"Oh," she said, barely a whisper. "Oh, no, Noah. I thought I could love him, or I wouldn't have considered courting him. The excitement of the beach almost fooled me into thinking I *did* love him, but I knew deep down that was a mistake. Now, after learning exactly what he's capable of, all I want is to be as far away from him as possible."

Noah didn't hesitate. "What if he repents? What if he asks forgiveness? You know that's what keeps a community strong when things like this happen."

Wide-eyed, Clara looked up at him. "Things like *this?* Not only did he ask to court me under false pretenses, he didn't know his wife was going to die. That means he would've married *me* while he was still married to *her*."

Wiping his eyes and nose, Vernon stood. Hay clung to his pants. His complexion resembled a storm over the Atlantic: dark, pulsing, dangerous. "I know it doesn't make any difference, but I divorced my wife a year after I left, so it wouldn't have been adultery if we had married."

"You're right, it wouldn't have made any difference," Noah said, trying to keep his temper under control. "In God's eyes, divorce is a construct of man, not Him. In His eyes, you were still married to her until she died. That means it still would've been adultery." Noah paused at a worse thought. "And worse than that, you *knew* it."

Vernon took his hat from the hay where it had fallen and clamped it over his head. "Clara, all I want is your happiness. I'm going home to write two letters of resignation to our community. One will be that I'm leaving for personal reasons. The other, which will be for you, will tell word for word what I did. All I ask is for you to keep it. I promise you here and now I'll never marry." He shook his head. "Can you imagine what it was like to be married to a woman who just sat in a chair all day, pulling strands of her own hair out? She would slap her parents when they walked by, curse them terribly with words she shouldn't have known. The doctors couldn't help and I couldn't help. I was doomed to a life without a wife, without love, without children. God help me. God help me. As soon as I can sell my house, I'll leave and never come back. All I want now is to stay Beachy Amish and live by myself. If I have to spend the rest of my life without the love of a fine woman like you to prove my repentance, so be it."

Noah noticed how Vernon didn't say he would like to ask his congregation for forgiveness. This meant he might not truly be sorry for his sins—from over a ten-year span at that. The right thing to do was to tell his congregation and let them vote on shunning him, but his story cut Noah's heart as if it had been his own. If the same thing happened to him, might he have acted in the same manner because of his desire to have a life filled with love? It was more than possible, so he couldn't see forcing Vernon from the church, but he couldn't stay here either. Thank goodness he had already offered to leave. Noah faced him. "You really plan on staying Beachy Amish?"

"I … I shouldn't, but I'd like to," Vernon said, his voice quavering. "Despite my wickedness, I don't consider myself evil. If I can be a help to only one soul for the rest of my life, it'll be worth it." He paused. His chest heaved in and out. "Are my terms acceptable to both of you? If you ever hear of me doing anything like this again, you'll always have that second letter to stop it—and me."

"How will we know where you are?" Clara asked.

"I'll call with my location." Vernon swallowed, licked his lips. "I know it's hard to trust me, but—"

"I trust you," Noah said. "I think you're really sorry." He glanced at Clara, hoping she could see how much he loved her in his eyes. "I can't imagine not having someone to love for the rest of my life either." He faced Vernon. "I have your phone number and you have mine. Call when you're settled, wherever that is. I—and maybe Clara too—would like to know you got there safely."

Vernon pressed his hand to his eyes, let out a single sob, and lowered his hand. "Thank you—both of you. I don't deserve your charity or your trust. It means more to me than I can say." Without another word, he strode quickly to his car. Seconds later, it faded down the road.

Clara sat on the milking stool again. Noah said nothing, simply let her take in everything that had happened.

Out of sight in the yard, chickens clucked. In the pasture beside the barn, the cow lowed softly. Bluebirds warbled, visible in the tree by Clara's porch.

Noah wondered how many times she and Abram had listened to them? How many times had they remarked on the colors, both of orange breast feathers and powder-blue wings, backs, and tails? How many times had they kissed beneath that tree, so in love, so happy, until she lost him two years ago come next March?

Noah knelt by Clara, looked into her eyes, dared a grin. "Maybe I should rent Vernon's house from him. That way I can keep up with his location from where I send the check."

Clara sputtered laughter. "Thank you for that. I know I've criticized you for your teasing at times, but I needed a laugh to help get over this mess." Gripping his arm, she stood. "I know you were joking about renting Vernon's house, but it would be nice if you stayed a while. I can use a friend. If anything, I know you're a friend. You saved me from who knows how much heartache. Vernon might've talked me into marrying him regardless of my misgivings. You know how we Beachy Amish value family and community."

Noah marveled at her hand gently gripping his arm. Such a simple touch might mean her old affection for him was returning, if only in gratitude for bringing the truth about Vernon to light. "Do you really want me to stay? You know I will if you want me to."

She nodded. "Yes, I do. Not that you want to join our community, but we need new members. We're dwindling to almost nothing, and we'll need a new bishop with Vernon leaving."

Noah laughed out loud. "Oh no, I'm not bishop material. I'm too jokie for that."

Clara released his arm. "We'll figure it out. Samuel—she's Alison's husband—I told you about her at the beach—has mentioned being a deacon. If everyone agrees, he can fill in until we find a candidate for a bishop."

The unmistakable sound of a screen door squeaking came from toward the house, then slammed, followed by the pattering of children's feet toward the barn. A little boy and girl peeked into the barn door, eyes questioning Noah's presence.

Clara waved them over. "John, Edna, this is Noah. He's an old friend from when I used to live with Grandpa and Grandma. I knew him before I met your papa."

Noah knelt before the two precious children. "It's nice to meet you. I'm going to be staying nearby for a while, I hope. Do you think we can be friends?"

John eyed him. "Do you like to fish?"

"Or ride in a boat?" Edna asked. "We like fishing and riding in a boat."

"A pontoon boat," John added. "Like Jonah took us in that time." He looked up at Clara. "Right, Mama?"

"That's exactly right."

Noah stood and faced Clara. "Jonah drove you and the children to your parent's house last year, right?"

"He did." Clara pointed over a grassy hill, where several black angus beef cattle were grazing. "He's my neighbor. He lives right over that hill in that house."

"Oh, that's right," Noah said. "I met him yesterday. I don't think I knew he lives right beside you."

Clara touched his arm. "If you haven't eaten, would you like some breakfast? You can see Jonah's work in the kitchen then."

"He gave us a washer," Edna said.

"And a 'frigerator," John said.

"*Re*-frigerator," Edna corrected.

"Now, now," Clara said. "No arguing if you want pancakes."

John and Edna darted to the house. The screen door slammed behind them, leaving no doubt about their love for pancakes.

"They're a mess," Noah said. "I'm sure they were a comfort when you lost Abram."

Clara's gaze moved from the barn door opening, past the house, and rose as she lifted her chin. It seemed that Jonah's house, just over the hill, drew her attention more than if he were something besides a driver, an electrician, and a friend.

"Is Jonah married?" Noah asked.

"His—" Clara's chin lowered. Her eyelids fluttered several times, as if she were questioning what she was about to say. "His sister Lydia lives with him. You know how some Amish groups don't care to socialize with the English. Since our community is far away and so small, Vernon gave me permission to allow Jonah to help me with plowing the garden and with other chores I couldn't do by myself." She paused. "He's … he's very special to me. If it hadn't been for him taking Edna to the hospital in South Boston when a Black

Widow spider bit her …"

As her voice trailed off, Noah understood. "You might've lost Edna like you lost Abram. I'm glad Jonah was there for you." Noah looked over the hill at the house. Regardless of Jonah being English, could he be a rival for Clara's love? *Nonsense*, he thought. *She's a proper Beachy Amish Mennonite woman who wouldn't dream of such a thing.*

He snapped his fingers. "Let me catch Vernon and see if he'll rent me the house. As fast as he left here, he's in a hurry to leave, so maybe he'll do that and sell it later."

Clara gripped his arm again. "I hope he will. Thank you for caring enough to tell me about him." In one swift movement, she raised on tiptoe and kissed his cheek, then dropped to her heels smiling and hurried inside, the blue dress flapping around her legs.

In his car, as he drove toward Nathalie, Noah pressed his hand to his chest. Yes, his heart was still beating. He hadn't died and gone to Heaven and dreamed of Clara kissing him, even if it was only a chaste kiss to his cheek.

Beaming a smile into the rear-view mirror, he winked. "Thank you, Lord, for your many blessings. If you will, please grant me the blessing of marrying Clara and being a father to her children within the next year. Amen."

Chapter 16

Three weeks later, when the shock of Vernon leaving the community had lessened, Clara, having carried Edna to Alison's for school, decided on a walk around the farm. John said he would be okay inside with a coloring book.

Although the late October breeze, cool and crisp, chilled her, it was a pleasant sensation, adding the herbal aroma of the leaves in the woods on the back border of the farm where she strolled, transforming into their fall colors. Hearing the tentative crunch of an animal's footfalls, she stopped beside a huge oak. More footfalls, each closer, announced a whitetail buck with mating on his mind. Clara had seen deer before on the farm, but never this close, eating acorns just within the trees. He raised his head to crash antlers against a low limb; acorns and leaves scattered around him in flashes of yellow and orange. Clara didn't know whether to giggle or fuss about his attitude, similar to Jonah's whenever he talked of his guitar lessons with Tess. Like this buck, now pawing the ground to leave a calling card for a doe, he would raise his hands to show anyone who would watch how he placed his fingers on the guitar, both on its neck and by its strings, to play a tune.

The breeze shifted. The buck stamped the ground, blew a snort of warning, and whirled away, its white tail flagging through the trees.

Jonah had a cookout recently; of course he invited Tess. He claimed to have invited Denver and Eliza, so Lydia told Alison, but Clara doubted it. Another story relayed to Alison by Lydia explained how Tess had invited Denver to the Woodbine Vineyard, a few miles west of Clarksville, to watch her perform with the guitar. During one song, she had even insisted he come on stage while she sang *I Only Have Eyes for You* to him. Naturally he sang the words back to her, surprising everyone with his deep baritone singing voice.

The news had both saddened and enlightened Clara. It saddened her because his confession of having feelings for her not long after they met was no more. It enlightened her because his seeing Tess meant Lydia was his sister and not his fiancé, as Alison had rumored back then as well. But that news had saddened Clara too. If Lydia was his sister, and Clara ever had cause to leave the Beachy Amish, God forbid, they could've seen where their affection could've taken them. Now that chance was gone, blown away by the wind like a golden shower of leaves from a hickory tree.

Clara had taken to writing poetry lately, and her latest, written when the realization that she must say goodbye to the possibility of marrying Jonah forever, whispered to her on the chilly breeze.

Whether I give of myself or not,
Whether I give or receive love or not,
I have loved and will love again.
God will not abandon me.
He is my strength,
My redeemer,
The One who knows my every need.
Like the bluebirds in spring,
When their song foretells of nestlings,
I will mouth my words of faith to You, O Lord,
For only faith will bring the one I am meant to love,
For all my life to come.

As Clara walked back to the house through wisps of grass up to her knees, grasshoppers whirred before her, scattering with clattering wingbeats, long hind legs dangling. Beneath the oak, Abram's white cross beckoned. He had gifted her more than love; he had gifted her two wonderful children to comfort her on chilly autumn winter nights as they cuddled in bed to be read some of the simpler verses from the Bible, paving the way for more serious truths.

Colossians 3:20: Children, obey your parents in all things: for this is well pleasing unto the Lord.

Hearing this verse, Edna always looked up at Clara with narrowed eyes. "Obey in *all* things? What if I meet a boy you don't like?"

Psalms 107:1: O give thanks unto the LORD, for he is good: for his mercy endureth forever.

Nodding, John always said, "That's right, Mama, like Papa's mercy. He didn't fuss like you do when I track mud in the kitchen."

During these sweet times, warmed by their small bodies, Clara never said anything; she just smiled with gratitude for God's many blessings—and for the blessing of the short time she had shared with her kind and gentle Abram.

About to go into the kitchen, she heard a hummingbird's wings whir around the corner of the house. She had put away the feeder, the tiny flying emeralds having left for South America in September. She followed the sound, hopping off the end of the porch, but it faded as if it had never existed.

Over the hill between her and Jonah's farm, he raised a hand in the distance as he stood amongst his beef cattle: a bluejeaned and white-shirted blur with chestnut brown hair.

Clara's breath hung in her throat. It was only a matter of time before Noah asked her to court him, and he deserved every consideration.

As she raised her hand toward Jonah, regret cut her soul to ribbons.

Dear Lord, you know my heart like you know every hummingbird's wingbeat. If You have led me around the house to see my destiny, I will be forever grateful.

To her left, gravel crunched at the end of the driveway, followed by the whir of hummingbird wings fading toward Noah as he drove toward her, his hand waving out the window.

Destiny.

Love.

Following God's will.

One way or another, whether on hummingbird wings or in prayer, Clara intended to discover the one man she was meant to love for the rest of her life.

Amen.

Readers: please enjoy the first chapter of the final book in the Clara Engelman Series, *Clara's Choice*, to be published later this year.

Standing at the podium, Samuel faced the community members gathered around the living room. "Welcome to our Sunday service. I'd like to start with a verse to remind us of the beauty of spring, which just came yesterday according to the calendar." He opened his Bible. "Isaiah 55:12. For ye shall go out with joy, and be led forth with peace: the mountains and the hills shall break forth before you into singing, and all the trees of the field shall clap their hands. Let us pray."

Clara closed her eyes. She was sitting with John and Edna on one of the benches at the kitchen table. Beside John sat Noah, now a member of the community, having joined three months after Vernon left last year in October. The news had both shocked and appeased Clara's parents. Both had hoped Noah would court and marry Clara and bring her home to be near them, but they were happy to hear that Vernon had seen the light, so to speak, with how he and Clara weren't a good match, which was what Clara had told them. As always, she regretted lying, but she had promised to keep Vernon's lies about his wife a secret. His story of her mental illness and how it had affected his life deserved forgiveness. God, of course, had already forgiven Clara's sin of lying, for he knew her heart and why she had done so. Vernon had suffered enough. He had seen the error of his ways and should be allowed to serve God in another community.

Samuel finished his prayer and raised his head. "It's good to have Jonah, Lydia, and Tess join us today. As we have decided by vote when they asked about coming, we won't turn away anyone from hearing God's word whether they are English or Amish. Now, the message today will also come from Isaiah 55:12."

As Samuel continued, Clara could hear the soft breaths of Jonah, Lydia, and Tess on the bench behind her. Although Jonah and Lydia had come to the Sunday service once a month since October, this was Tess's first visit since he had started taking guitar lessons from her last September. According to Alison, Lydia said the lessons now included regular visits to her Tess's home. So far, though, the visits seemed innocent enough, spent fishing from her dock or going out to supper in Clarksville, but the chance of romance with her must've been on Jonah's mind.

To Clara's left, John fidgeted. Patting his knee,

Noah caught her eye and winked. His delay in asking to court her was a surprise. Not only had he saved her from a marriage with Vernon, he was now renting Vernon's home north of Nathalie. Acting more like a big brother than a potential beau, he visited Clara and the children once a week or so, saying he wanted to make sure they didn't need anything done around the house. Although his delay in asking to court her was a surprise, she attributed it to his understanding of how she needed time to get over the blow of how Vernon had lied to her.

From behind Clara, the faint aroma of perfume came from Tess. Lydia had never worn it that Clara had noticed, odd for English women. Perhaps Tess wore it for Jonah, trying to attract him like a bee to a flower. As much time as they spent together, he was more like a spider caught in her web.

Clara knew she shouldn't but she envied Tess's full figure. Compared to her, Clara looked like a skinny scarecrow. No wonder Jonah was attracted to her. At least she was wearing a blue, knee-length skirt and a white sweater with a neckline well above her cleavage to the service. If not Samuel might not be able to keep his eyes averted, especially from her lustrous auburn hair flowing over her shoulders and down her back. Yes, Jonah must be smitten, so how long before he proposed to her?

Taking in a labored breath, Clara hated the thought of Jonah married. Since she had realized she loved him—no, she was *in* love with him—her days and nights had been spent trying to purge him from her mind. Noah's visits helped, but always, whether gathering eggs, milking the cow, or doing any other farm chore, that night in Pennsylvania, when they had gone on a drive, haunted her with his living presence. He must've sensed her unease about courting Vernon, or he wouldn't have called her from his hotel room to start with. Then, when they had parked by a river and she had brazenly crawled into his lap with her hair down like a child to be comforted, she had felt nothing like a child. Those few moments had been intimate but not. Although he held her close, it was the embrace of a friend when she'd rather he embrace her as a man.

That night was gone and never would return. It was time to look past Jonah and consider Noah as a husband, plus the father John and Edna needed.

Clara caught snippets of Samuel's sermon, thoughts of Jonah and Tess as distracting as an annoying fly. Behind her, Tess whispered something to Jonah and he whispered back. Words of love? A proposal at this very moment?

Samuel closed the Bible. "I hope no one minds if my sermon isn't as long as it should be. I'm still trying to get the hang of preaching. Let's stand and sing *How Great Thou Art*. Then we'll have the blessing and enjoy this fine meal the ladies prepared.

Everyone stood and sang. Jonah and Tess, no doubt, preferred to play guitar to accompany the voices, but that was never voted on in this congregation. Behind Clara, their rich voices joined as one, aggravating Clara even more. *Really*, she thought, *like the English say, you two should get a room.*

The song ended. Samuel said the blessing. At the table, the ladies uncovered bowls and platters, releasing the aromas of chicken, beef, and pork, either in individual dishes or in casseroles with gravy oozing around the sides. A line formed. Plates were filled with green beans, boiled potatoes, beets, buttered rolls, and slices of meat. Eyes darted at vanilla crumb pie, apple fritter bread, and sugar cookies, all waiting to be served for dessert.

Clara filled the children's plates. They went outside to join Alison's boys, who were sitting with their plates in their laps and their feet dangling off the porch. Noah was standing in a corner with Samuel. They alternated between talking and eating from the plates they held in one hand, a fork in the other. Lydia, Alison, and Tess were huddled in a corner of the kitchen, their plates on a counter. The rest of the small community sat in chairs, chatting between bites and sips of lemonade.

Tess joined Clara at the table and filled a glass with lemonade. "Alison sure loves to gossip. Before Lydia came over, she wanted to know if Jonah and I were dating."

Clara wanted to know that very thing herself. "Well, I wouldn't call it gossip if there's truth in it."

Tess sipped lemonade. Jonah had walked over to Samuel and Noah. His huge smile suggested he was talking about playing the guitar.

"I don't understand why some lucky girl hasn't snagged Jonah yet?" Tess turned from him to face Clara. "Do you?"

Sipping lemonade, Clara lowered the glass. "I was hoping you could tell me why, as much time as you spend with him."

Tess's full lips, shaded with pink lipstick, fought with what resembled a smile and a frown. "I'm not the one watching him so intently. I understand he's been a great help to you around the farm. He's told me a lot about you and he and Lydia and your children since we met during your camping trip at Occoneechee State Park. It's Clara this and Clara that, John this and Edna that. To hear him talk, he would like to be their dad."

Clara clenched her teeth. No doubt Tess would

rather have him be a dad to *her* children. "What's Denver doing while you're here?" Clara's character didn't let her say the rest: *I understand you and Eliza trade him on weekends.*

"They're home from church by now. We attend a country church not too far outside of Clarksville."

Lydia came over. "Well, ladies, what do you think of these handsome Amish farmhands?" She nodded toward the corner with Jonah, Samuel, and Noah. "Especially Noah. If I tried, I bet I could make him leave your little community to marry me."

Drinking lemonade again, Clara swallowed before she strangled herself. The audacity of such a statement was beyond belief.

Tess laughed. "He's handsome all right, but my Jonah has them *all* beat." She looked at Clara. "Don't you think so?"

Carrying a slice of vanilla crumb pie, Alison hurried over. "I heard that. I know I'm supposed to say my Samuel is the handsomest man here, but I could eat Jonah up like this pie."

More audacity, and from Clara's best friend at that. Rather than shame her friend, Clara left for the porch. The screen door squeaked behind her, followed by another squeak. "I saw you talking to Tess," Jonah said. "She's something else, isn't she?"

"She sure is, for a woman who trades her sister's

husband every other weekend."

Jonah laughed. "You and your jokes. Besides, you know better than that. She explained their situation when we met them on our camping trip in the park." He stepped around in front of her and looked her in the eye. "Enough of that. I keep expecting to hear about you courting Noah."

Clara took a step backward. "I keep expecting to hear you're going marry Tess, as much time as you spend with her."

Jonah grinned. "Well, the idea is tempting. I love her Dutch accent from when she and her family were Amish in Ohio. Eliza's story is amazing, falling in love with Denver when he was her sign language teacher and becoming a famous artist. That's as romantic as romantic gets."

With hot tears welling at her confused feelings, Clara whirled around and faked a sneeze. "I think I'm catching a cold," she said, taking a handkerchief from her pocket.

The screen door squeaked open. "A cold?" Noah asked.

"Maybe," she said. "I should get the children in the pickup and get home before I spread it around."

"Your nose isn't even stuffy," Jonah said.

Noah tilted his head to one side. "If she said she has a cold, Jonah, she has a cold. I'll get your dishes and put them in the truck, Clara. Jonah, maybe you can nice enough to get the children in the truck."

As Noah went inside, Jonah looked into Clara's eyes again. "I apologize, Clara, if you are sick." He paused. "I was only teasing about Noah. I'm not sure if he can make you as happy as Abram did. I hope you know all I want is for you to be happy."

Nodding, Clara ducked her head. "I know. Thank you." A sudden thought raised her eyes to his. "You never wired the rest of the house last fall. Do you think you can before the summer heat gets here? Air conditioning sounds wonderful."

"Yeah. My herd coming down with Foot Rot had me as busy as I could be. Thank the Lord they're doing okay now."

Carrying two covered plates, Noah opened the screen door. "I'll get this and the children in the truck. I see your neighbor isn't going to do it."

Jonah eyed him as he strode toward John and Edna, kicking a ball with Alison's boys. Clara touched his sleeve. "I'm sorry I was short with you. Do you know how we get in bad moods sometimes and don't know why?"

"I do exactly. I'll stop by tomorrow and look over the house again. I need to make a list of all the supplies we need. Right now I'll try a slice of that vanilla crumb pie."

"See you tomorrow." Clara watched him go inside. At the pickup, Noah waved her over and opened the door for her.

After she climbed in, he shut the door and leaned his elbows on the window opening. "I'm going to drive to Pennsylvania this week after I plant my garden and see my folks." He tipped his wide-brimmed straw hat back, revealing blond hair and blue eyes.

For Clara, those features didn't hold the same charm they had when they were teenagers. "Have a safe trip. If you see my folks, tell them I hope to visit soon."

Noah said he would and left for his pickup, which he had traded his car for not long after he rented Vernon's house. It seemed he was putting roots down in southern Virginia for good. Considering his and Clara's past, she knew why.

Now to get home and plan the planting of her own garden. Not wanting to go back inside, she made a mental note to call Alison tonight and apologize for leaving without saying goodbye.

She just didn't feel like facing Tess again.

ABOUT THE AUTHOR

J. Willis Sanders lives in southern Virginia, with his wife and several stringed musical instruments.

With sixteen books completed and more on the way, he enjoys crafting intriguing characters with equally intriguing conflicts to overcome. He also loves the natural world and, more often than not, his stories include those settings. Most also utilize intense love relationships and layered themes.

His first idea for a novel is a ghostly World War II era historical that takes place mostly in the midwestern United States, which utilizes some little-known facts about German POW camps there at the time. It's the first of a three-book series, in which characters from the first continue their lives.

Although he loves history, he has written several contemporary novels as well, and some include interesting paranormal twists, both with and without religious themes.

He also loves the Outer Banks of North Carolina, and he has written three novels within different time frames based on the area, what he calls his Outer Banks of North Carolina Series. As of

January 2023, he's writing another novel about the area.

And yes, he enjoys learning about the variations of Amish culture, which inspired his Eliza Gray and Clara Engelman series.

Other hobbies include reading (of course), vegetable gardening, playing music with friends, and songwriting, some of which are in a few of his novels.

To follow his work, visit any of these websites:

https://jwillissanders.wixsite.com/writer

https://www.facebook.com/J-Willis-Sanders-874367072622901

https://www.amazon.com/J-Willis-Sanders/e/B092RZG6MC?ref_=dbs_p_ebk_r00_abau_000000

Readers: to help those considering a purchase, please leave a review on Amazon.com, Goodreads.com, or wherever you bought this book. They help authors more than you may realize.